QUINCY

A NOVEL BY

EVERETT HEATH

Reader House Publishing
Quincy©
Cover Design: Model-T Digital

Everett Heath

Everett was born in Texas.

He spent much of his childhood in Europe before returning to the United States.

After living in Alaska for some time, Everett now lives in Hawaii.

Chapter 1

"We block our own way, don't you think? That's why I want to be here—in a place where there's little to block my way. Maybe I can at least wipe spittle from their lips. Of course, I can't forget all those who will rely on me to pray for them. But, is that enough?"

As far as Quincy Lane was concerned, her interview was over. She knew to say no more; otherwise she'd go deep. This may be life changing. That's how Quincy interpreted Stephen's request. Keep the smile genuine--be attentive. Listen. She knew what a life coach would preach, nauseating as *they* were.

In this final interview, Father Ash Price was no longer shocked by Quincy Lane. Not anymore. She fatigued him. More than any demanding resident living here. He didn't interview Quincy--she interviewed herself. He imagined finishing today by saying to her, 'You're not what this residence seeks.' But he knew he would be unable to resisting adding, '...at all.'

Plus, a flogging reminder that he failed in his attempt to ignore the fact that along with Quincy came an unimaginable amount of money. He did not trust one cell of Quincy's being. Even more so because he knew she could see through his smile—and straight to his righteous irritation to her presence.

Quincy told herself that she hated having money come into play. She smiled when she told herself the best lies. She wanted to believe, she more or less wanted to have faith. But when beauty retires and power wanes, belief in wealth and possession of much of it--always wins in the end.

Quincy said, "You didn't ask me any questions."

"You seem to provide all the answers to questions anyone would think to ask," said Father Price.

"You doubt my sincerity?"

"I do not doubt your sincerity," he said.

He rose from his desk, spotless and free of anything at all, save Quincy's parting reflection in the polished surface as she rose from her chair. Father Price shook her hand and thanked her for her sincere interest in being a resident. Quincy smiled and allowed him to escort her out of the office.

"I'll call you soon," he said.

From across the courtyard Grace tipped his brown stingy brim fedora. Quincy, escorted by Father Price, took notice, and she smiled in return. They turned into a walkway that led to the small parking lot out in front of the residence. The taxi had been waiting ten minutes. Grace hustled across the courtyard to catch another glimpse of Quincy, only to see the taxi driving away. Grace owned three suits and seven white shirts. He could afford to sweat stain the flyaway shirt collars and replace them every week if necessary. He wore a suit every day, only on occasion did he wear a tie. No one could predict those occasions. Both pairs of his brown leather shoes were polished to a shimmering shine. For a man out of mental sorts, he knew a thing or two about how to dress.

'Out of mental sorts' was his invention. Sometimes he allowed himself a moment to feel pride of this fact, since many living here now used the term. Yes, epileptic seizures bent his brain, his cognition compromised, but his ability to take care of himself only came into occasional doubt. Grace chose to live in the residence, and the weight of his family's relief surpassed a mile-long string of boxcars crammed with bars of gold, an amount they would offer on the sunniest of days to ransom their freedom of him--for that was the wealth of his family and the weight of their annoyance of his presence.

But Father Price refused the ransom--and accepted Gordie 'Grace' Smalls into the residence for a maintenance fee, plus his exotically expensive drug requirements, and full hospital care, in the event Mr. Smalls required such care. Only Father Price knew his real name. When Gordie arrived, he only referred to himself as Grace. He was not as damaged as one could observe, and a difficult man to know well. He surprised with regularity. He was invaluable.

The numbers in the address of the residence added together equaled the total number of those who resided here. Coincidence in numbers fascinated Peter, but he could only pronounce his name as Petrol. He and Grace were not the only ones out of mental sorts. The others were women. Neither Grace nor Petrol considered Jane a woman, despite his intimidations. Grace said that Jane limited himself by methodical abuse, trying to stay happy through a variety of potent drugs, whereas God had limited the other residents--for His own reasons.

The residence was a failed attempt for the cognitively disabled. It began as a limited experiment, privately funded, to get those without any support into an established religious community to provide full assistance. Those that could survive on the streets never stayed put. They wanted no part of the residence, regardless of religion. Those that could not survive did not exist. Father Price took over from an ex bureaucrat who was removed from his previous post for being lousy. Father Price asked for no salary or budget, and he was hired on the spot. It became known he was seeking residents. Word got out to those families in the region who still cared for their own. Some found a new home for their sons and daughters. He changed the name to the Life Boat.

Vanier had L'Arche.
Price had the Life Boat.
Unlike Father Price's previous endeavors, he was all in this time. Full commitment. And unlike his previous endeavors, he had to succeed. He had to.

In the middle of the courtyard, Grace sat alone, sweating in the high sun. Memories were stacked tall here in this place, thought Grace, not aware his own memories were like small piles of soft bricks sorted by shape, consistency, and color--in a large field, slowly crumbling well before their time. His imagination was never inhibited however, as he imagined students scurrying through the inside perimeter arcade on a Friday afternoon, just before the school day ended, with barking nuns directing traffic. But there were no more nuns. The former classrooms were situated below, and on the second floor were bedrooms of the nuns who taught here, way back then. The Arabic arched arcade leading to their rooms was on the outside perimeter, with each room having a large obscured glass window looking into the courtyard, and outward, a large clear window looking beyond the school grounds. Grace called the courtyard facing windows, 'stained glass without the stain.' He had no opinions about nuns, one way or the other. The Catholic school never had a chance, like a sushi restaurant in a dying desert town nowhere close to the ocean.

On Sunday morning Quincy pulled into the small parking lot of the Life Boat. She thought the name was ridiculous. She noticed the crumbling asphalt. The parking lot was filled with automobiles. The day was already hot, the drought was on, and attesting were the few remaining spindly weeds that had poked through the cracks in the asphalt in a brief victory over man—an ironic testament to nature. They were bent over, brown and dead. All the more reason to select a white colored van, she thought, squinting through her sunglasses at the rising sun, and then at the parking lot filled with automobiles. Quincy purchased a fully loaded van, but she kept her Bentley. Entering the courtyard, she noticed how green and cared for was the grass. It was cool in the arcade as she looked for any one up and about. There were no weeds growing amongst the flagstones that formed the arcade floor. The residence was still. Father Price's office was empty. Quincy opened two doors around the opposite side and those rooms too were empty. At the opposite end of the courtyard an archway led to an opening behind the main building. To the right, within the tall chain linked fence surrounding the back of the property was a small field, also green, and well tended. Beyond the fence lay hardened dirt, patches and clumps of dried shrubs, weeds, and anything else that could attempt to survive in drought. To the left, was a small chapel of white plaster—the same as the main building. She listened, leaning her ear close to the front entrance chapel door. Either solid construction or empty, she thought. She opened the door very slow. There was no creaking sound but the ten rows of pews were filled with people—all turning their heads around to look at Quincy as Father Price pronounced from the altar, "The Mass has ended, go in peace to love and serve the Lord." The faces in the chapel matched the cars in the parking lot. Old, well preserved, and money not an issue. Stephen told her he was amazed how church goers could always find a priest—anywhere. Chalk one up for the Catholic Church. Quincy entered as the congregation left the church, only a couple of women acknowledging Quincy's presence. The rest filed out of the chapel. The few remaining were in the front pews. Among them were also Grace and Petrol. Father Price returned from the sacristy in jeans and a short sleeved collared shirt. He noticed Quincy the moment she peered inside the chapel. She wore fitted grey slacks and a beige sleeveless blouse and a tiny silver cross on a short chain around her neck.

"Father, I'm saving you the time calling me. I'd prefer to hear your decision face to face, adding with a smile, "And in a chapel no less!"

"No surprise to see you here this early Mrs. Lane," he said, not altogether true, but preempting her maneuver to pressure him otherwise if his decision was not favorable to her desire. He knew it was more a demand to become a resident assistant than a desire. More calculating than seeking. More inclined to claim something than to offer anything. Humility was a complete foreign antibody to her being, thought Price, and she seemed to be on cordial terms with truculence, if pressed. At that moment, both chapel doors were opened and the morning's rays blinded everyone, save Quincy, who still wore her dark sunglasses. Grace and Petrol were holding the doors as those remaining walked down the aisle towards the exit. They were the five women residents and their visiting families. Father Price nodded and said goodbye to them all. Quincy stood next to Father Price and smiled, observing.

"Louisa, tall Mary Osborne, short Mary, Veronica, and Monique," whispered Grace to Quincy.

"But who is who?" she asked. Grace tipped his fedora slightly right, grabbed her hand and together they followed behind those remaining; pointing and describing each by height, weight and color of clothing, and style of wheelchair. Father Price and Petrol closed the chapel doors and soon followed, with Petrol's arm held firm by Father Price.

Chapter 2

All of the visiting family were now in Father Price's office, and with them on the long taupe sofa, were Louisa, tall Mary, short Mary, Veronica and Monique. Two empty wheel chairs were collapsed and placed behind the sofa. The mother of short Mary was also short, and loud, and shaped like a squashed bowling pin. Her face was flush, which did not match her floral dress, thought Quincy. She stood with the families, because Grace insisted. As Father Price entered his office, the mother of short Mary stood up her chair and announced,

"Father Price, we have decided, and now firmly insist you bring in a woman resident assistant-- immediately."

Quincy observed the women sitting on the sofa, trying to guess their names by their looks and facial expressions. This proved to be difficult for they all displayed minimal expression, and everyone but tall Mary looked up and watched Father Price go to his desk and sit down. The rest of the women seemed to have other things more interesting to look at in their laps or on the ceiling.

Father Price was not pleased. And if ordered to prioritize the list of his displeasures he would fail, because so many were number one. He allowed himself an internal chuckle at that moment, aware of his hand in his own fate, chuckling at the absurd difficulty in identifying the number one.

"Anyone care for refreshments? Coffee? Flavored water? Diet soda?" asked Father Price, now tipping his head in a slight manner towards the mother of short Mary, adding, "You are always welcome here, and thank you for sharing your concern." A few of the family raised their hands and asked for coffee. Looking around the office his eye caught Quincy who then asked,

"Where is the coffee?"

Grace wasted no time leading her through a side door to the break room, where a pot of coffee was waiting, just as it was every morning. Quincy found a tray and placed on it four cups, coffee creamer and sweetener, and finally the coffee pot. It rested on top of a handmade cast iron trivet, with the San Francisco Bridge as the design. Low conversation quieted as Quincy re-entered Father Price's office. She served coffee and returned to the break room to fetch two bottled waters and three flavored waters for the others who decided just then they were thirsty.

"Well Father, your Dr. Olivia has been gone ten days now. She was your last female on staff. You don't know when she is returning, so you have said. Maybe she won't return. But we do know our girls need a female around. More than one--I might suggest at least three. No females? Father, that's not right. And I personally am not so sorry to say that Mr. Jane does not count."

Although, thought Father Price, in the time he had been here, not one of the women residents ever displayed any apprehension with Jane. Every Life Boat woman was fond of Jane. It was obvious to everyone Jane was not present this morning. Today was grocery and sundries shopping day. It was also his day away from the Life Boat. In a typical sun dress, he returned about four pm, unloading and putting away all the purchases, and then planned dinner. How he managed to get a driver's license and complete his tasks were a small-scale miracle. Jane's brain was broken but he succeeded every shopping day. Getting him to go to Mass first was another challenge.

Father Price believed in miracles--but didn't believe in coincidences, in his mind their appearances were only man made. But this morning's activity briefly tempted his belief in both. Quincy had to be accepted; otherwise the situation would be elevated and then beyond his control. Father Price was not pleased. And he missed Dr. Olivia Pernell in more ways than he should.

Chapter 3

"You play guitar?" asked Tall Mary.

"No, I don't," replied Quincy. Tall Mary pouted.

"I play bass," said Tall Mary, now smiling.

"We are The Syndromes and we do not have a guitar in the band. Olivia played piano, but that is not guitar, and she's not here."

"You are in a band? With whom?" asked Quincy.

"Women only!" said Tall Mary.

"You mean Veronica, Louisa, and Short Mary?" asked Quincy.

"We are The Syndromes. I told you."

"Where did you get your name for your band?"

"We all have syndromes."

Quincy remained without expression, knowing she would laugh to tears later.

Tall Mary was six feet easy, and skinny as a rock and roller. Her gray hair was pulled back into a ponytail, well below her shoulders. She wore black, all the time. Her pajamas were black. But her lipstick was apple red. She always had been a rock and roller. She told that to everyone.

Together they watched the two Cynths clear away the dinner dishes from the table. These older versions were still mechanical in their movements but they were quiet and efficient and no longer did any of the residents have to do dishes. Their names where White and Gray. Tall Mary got up from table and left, offering a quick shy wave to White and Gray. They both stopped, and then resumed cleaning the table. Quincy watched Tall Mary leave and noticed she was knock kneed. There was some similarity to the Cynths in the way she walked.

Quincy now sat alone, sipping hot coffee, thanks to White. With her first day complete, Quincy felt fully confident she had made a mistake to live here. One day of keeping her thoughts to herself, and keeping her mouth shut except for courteous exchanges with everyone exhausted her into a funk. It was seven pm and now she had to tend to assisting the women in their evening ablutions. Tall Mary was not happy Quincy was now here to assist her bandmates, as she referred to them. Unless Quincy could learn how to play guitar. That would be different. Dr. Olivia at least played piano, so she was OK to help, even though she did not play guitar.

As Quincy assisted Tall Mary with the other women in getting them ready for bed, Quincy believed it would be easier to learn guitar than to give the attention these women required. Two had very little concept in hygiene, other than they knew they had released their bowls and urinated. Controlling themselves was only possible if reminded at the time they needed to go. And only tall Mary, short Mary, and Veronica could use the toilet unassisted. Monica had to have two baths per evening, because the first bath she would defecate and urinate soon after she was placed in the tub. Something about the warm water.

Every woman loved their comfortable chairs facing the window in order to look out, beyond the white chapel and green field in the back of the property, out to the gradual rise of elevation, towards the brown hills, and up to the mountains, bare of snow for so long.

Quincy finished her shower and sat on her single bed with the lights out. It was eight thirty pm and she opened her window. The room was bare. One large nightstand with an ample lamp, a four-door dresser of giveaway vintage, sturdy though, with deep drawers, a walk-in closet, a small desk and chair set with its own small lamp, fair quality for composite materials, a comfortable sitting chair, and a bathroom with insufficient lighting to properly apply any makeup. She thought again about the name of their band, The Syndromes. She also thought about Tall Mary and Short Mary. Those were ridiculous names as well.

Lying down now Quincy laughed, and then she cried, eyes staying open all night, finally falling asleep at dawn, only to be jolted awake less than an hour later by sounds that she could not begin to describe, other than being at war. She had just dreamt of an earthquake and standing on undulating ground, and when her eyes opened she knew she was going to look like half-baked hell all day.

****

On Saturdays there was no morning Mass. The sixth day of the week was the second least organized. Nothing scheduled except dinner and morning band practice. Clanging fits and starts was a good enough description of their sound, thought Quincy, or perhaps like a six year old holding on to a temper tantrum but getting tired of holding on. Clearly well, well beyond punk rock—which was about to celebrate its fifty-ninth anniversary. These thoughts made her feel much better. Most people knew a little bit about everything, enough to recite slices of facts without referencing their personal electronic devices. Everyone had a PED, many had them implanted, especially the young and the certain old types who were well beyond giving a shit, convinced that everything had been reduced to trivialities.

Quincy steered towards the kitchen. It was a sunny hot morning. The grass in the courtyard lawn twinkled from the last of the water droplets. The sprinkler heads had retreated to their holes. Now it was competition between evaporation and absorption. The greenness of the grass indicated absorption was a temporary victor. She passed the closed door of the practice room. Coffee first, she said to herself. The Cynth named White recognized Quincy as she entered and then returned to the kitchen. Moments later White emerged with a small pot of coffee and a porcelain-like coffee cup.

"Good morning Quincy—cream with coffee?" said White, in a male programmed voice that reminded her of every other Cynth she had heard.

"Morning White," she replied. The Cynths detected vocal tones and facial reactions.

"Sleep well, Quincy?" asked White.

"No cream White--and don't ask me about my night's sleep. Ever. Remember that."

"I will Quincy."

"Pass that along to Gray too."

"I will Quincy," said White.

Father Price entered the dining room and White took notice before returning to the kitchen.

"Good morning," he said.

"Morning Father," said Quincy. She sipped her coffee, having no need for him to sit down and join her. Father Price sat down opposite Quincy as White appeared with a coffee tray that included creamer.

17

White poured the coffee and Father Price added a few drops of cream. Not worth the effort, thought Quincy, as White topped off her cup.

"We'll be asking you to help Tall Mary in the morning as well as evening. It's sometimes more than she is able to manage. She is motivated on Saturdays as you can now understand," said Father Price, tilting his head towards the band practice room. On Quincy's list of hates, being told what to do almost ranked as high as being corrected.

"The Syndromes?" asked Quincy adding in a monotone, "Why not call them 'Wake the Dead?'"

"That's not the name they chose," he said.

"Tall Mary chose, you mean," said Quincy.

"They agreed to the name," said Father Price.

"Like hell they did," she replied.

Quincy asked, "Within this place—why so many stupid names? Tall and Short Mary, The Syndromes...and for God's sake, the Life Boat?"

She went on asking, "And seriously, Jane is permitted to drive a car?"

"Jane can only drive the auto-drive cars, not the self-drive."

Father Price got up from his seat, grabbing his coffee pot and cup.

"I can only take credit for the name of this residence. The other names you'll have to ask them.

The whole reason for you being here is interaction—we are a community."

"I also forgot to say yesterday—welcome to the Life Boat." He left and went to his office. He could not be duller, thought Quincy. Was he ever sharp?

****

Tall Mary wore her black bass guitar high to her chest, and was rocking her upper torso back and forth, just as the heavy metal guitarists do. She whipped her long gray hair forward and back to her own beat, her hair long enough to touch her feet. At apogee, her flipping gray mane made Tall Mary appear ten feet tall. Quincy wasn't sure how many different notes she was actually hitting but it seemed Tall Mary had no interest in timing. Not, however, due to any help from her band mates.

Quincy quickly closed the door. After her shock of seeing Tall Mary in full, Quincy's eardrums reacted in sharp pain. Everyone was wearing ear protection, the bulbous, over the head kind of ear protection used by the Navy when launching jets off the carrier deck. Everyone but Tall Mary. On a stool, Veronica sat behind a kick drum, snare, hi-hat, and ride cymbal, primarily pummeling the snare, and at no particular time stopping to stomp on the kick drum pedal and

19

switching to bang on the ride cymbal. The hi-hat stood untouched. Opposite Tall Mary sat Louisa and Short Mary on metal foldable chairs, each with three bongo drums in front of them mounted on a stand, each with different size drums. With both hands, Louisa banged on her drums, appearing to listen to no one else, and Quincy was surprised she could actually hear her drum beats. Short Mary sat and studied her drums, her hands resting on the surface, occasionally lifting a finger and placing it back down on the surface. Then she would lift her head up and look at Jane, sitting off to the side but in direct line of sight of Short Mary. Jane made instructional motions to hit the bongos with her palms. Jane then pointed at an empty seat next to him. On the seat was a pair of ear protectors. Quincy sat down and put them on. At least Tall Mary wasn't a sartorial dictator of a bandleader, observed Quincy, none of the other women wore anything black. But, maybe that was her intent.

Saturday morning at the Life Boat.

Chapter 4

Quincy didn't look forward to the advancing construction of the VacTrain. She didn't care one way or the other. But after almost three weeks here, she had an earnest appreciation for why Mary Osborne (Tall Mary) gave full priority to staring out her window in the evenings, alert for the glow of blow torches piercing the twilight as the workers finished the VacTrain line, not more than two miles away from the Life Boat. Vacuum tubes housed circular train cars, and they traveled in excess of seven hundred miles per hour. Natural gas runs automobiles. Inexpensive fuel abounds, and intolerantly abundant. Most transport trucks are auto-drive. Only the old classic muscle cars use gasoline—so cheap around the world but now burdened with heavy taxes in many areas. Modes of transportation in competition with each other. Both pretending to be the best for human kind, both pretending to free man and woman from whatever location bound them. Powerful illusions: freedom via super-fast transportation and liberated from the bondage of location. But the ability to travel at a moment's decision was eroding. And in between coasts the people were not at all pleased. But Mary Osborne was happy to know she could soon go to unvisited places long distances away, very fast. For her, that was freedom. She had never been anywhere.

Quincy had long forgotten how to be happy for anyone else--what was the compelling reason? She was, however, approaching an understanding of why Mary Osborne felt the way she did. An understanding that just might have been mistaken for being happy for somebody.

The sky was blue, the air was dry, and billowy clouds were precious when found. It was yet another drought in the California region, the last one ending only seven years ago. Rain was forecast in the mountains, maybe later in the day. But their water tank was full, thanks to the Environmentos losing control over the de-salinization industry. Trucks powered by natural gas delivered water everywhere it was scarce. No further pipe systems, just gas powered auto-drive trucks. The roads had never been in such superb condition.

After Mass, Quincy joined the remaining family members that would attend every Sunday morning. She served them coffee, flavored waters, Coca Cola, doughnuts and pastries. There was no one to talk with. Grace and Petrol were their own company. Jane spent time with Mary Osborne, and the rest of the residents weren't capable of conversation. She wanted to strangle White and Gray. She imagined how strangling them might be so much more enjoyable than disconnecting their power source. And Father Price...where his mind was could only be one place. He had that singular focus kind of look--and Quincy was unconvinced he was captivated in prayerful meditation, or even his quest for eternal salvation. She had a much more plausible theory.

The non-family attendees didn't linger after Mass. They got in their autos and went to wherever they lived. If Quincy had found any of them in the slightest bit interesting she would have persuaded them to linger. The age gap for sure, thought Quincy, all of them at least twenty years or so older, and none of them still motivated to be thin, attractive, and conscious of style. That letting go of oneself--Quincy could not tolerate in the least.

The lousy previous Life Boat director prohibited virtual reality entertainment. Father Price continued with the prohibition, not because he simply condemned the practice of VR entertainment--which he did (everything possible or fantasized was presented as entertainment), but because the rate and permanence of VR addiction had disrupted culture in certain pockets of the country to such an extent VR addicts were converted to the willingness to not function whereas those in the Life Boat were willing but unable to function. Accidiacs and Live the

Myth were the two most prevalent VR groups, recently achieving full rights status. The VR industry underwrote their livelihood. They had abandoned any involvement in any society endeavor, other than societal VR immersion into manufactured Myths—sedentary, live action, and subgenres of every sort. Within the Myths innumerable virtual personalities could be created, as well as many gender types. Hybrid gender creation was still popular, although it had peaked.

VR immersion was now the default treatment for those still remaining who were severely out of mental sorts. But Dr. Olivia Pernell would not abide, and Father Price would never go against her judgment in these matters. Only with sponsor approval could the Life Boat authorize alternate treatment. Non-sponsored, those with no family at all, or those who had been rejected by family, underwent VR immersion in Region Centers. The VR Industry underwrote the Region Centers—they were small operations and getting smaller. The families had to sign consent for treatment other than VR.

On-grid Cynths were used extensively in Region Centers. Off-grid Cynths were illegal. The Life Boat Cynths, White and Gray, were off-grid but programmed with narrow service functions. Evading

Regulator intervention was not difficult when using only a few Cynths.

The after Mass social was over. The families returned home and the residences were settling into Sunday morning routines. Typically, Father Price spent the rest of the morning until early evening celebrating Mass in nearby communities where priests had long been gone. This Sunday was an exception to find him still here. So far, he had done an outstanding job spending as little time around Quincy as possible. Challenging to do at the Life Boat, with little to do, aside from caring for the residents. Sitting on one of the sofas in his office, he sipped his second cup of coffee. As Quincy was finishing cleaning up he asked, "Why are you here? You can be anywhere."

He continued. "You have severe mental incapacity anywhere along your family line?

"Your husband's family?"

"Close friends?"

Quincy left his office to wipe down the sink and counter top of the adjacent break room. The temptation to exit through the other door and leave all Father Price's questions unanswered was peaking to a boil. But an argument was better than silence between them. When she returned to his office Father Price was surprised. Calm, Quincy sat next to him, close enough to touch. She looked in his eyes,

Father Price now sitting up in the sofa rather than slouching in its thick cushions.

Ignoring he had said more to her in the series of questions than almost two months she had been living here, Quincy replied, "Why are you here? Not serving Mass elsewhere today like you usually do? Did Dr. Pernell remain here while you were gone all Sunday?" Of course, he was sleeping with Olivia Pernell, she thought. Dr. Pernell's gone and that's why he's been looking like he's afflicted with a perpetual irritable bowel.

"And to your questions--no mental incapacity in my family and none that I'm aware of in my ex-husband's. You? Certainly, you have a family history of something, don't you?"

Quincy continued, "Really, why are *you* here at all? No place more in need of a priest than here?"
Father Price rose quickly saying, "Excuse me please, I have some correspondence to catch up with."
Quincy got up from the sofa. She untied the calico kitchen apron and tossed it on his desk.

"Sit down and talk to me," she demanded, ignoring her awareness it was more plea than demand.

"There's no laughter here, other than Grace and Petrol doing silly things. Did you put something in the holy water?"

"I have no one to talk to, that is, no one I can converse with," said Quincy. She sat back down on the other sofa. Father Price remained standing.

"Are you not the god damned director of the Life Boat? Then--isn't it your job, or your vocation, or your whatever-the-fuck calling to administer direction? To all of us, here? Not exclusive to just the residents, but to all of us? You fucking prick of a priest!"

He sat down—on the opposite sofa.

He said, "You realize even White and Gray avoid you as much as they are programmed to. They categorize you as unpleasant, which I'm certain is only because their programmers elected not to use another word choice to describe their experiences with you. You're category 10 on a 10 scale of unpleasantness."

"Nothing new Father, nothing new. My therapist says as much. I don't like Cynths around me, no matter how holy they are. Probably the holy Cynths are even more obnoxious. But I guess I shouldn't take it out on the robots, should I? Ok, their programmers then."

"And you categorize me at what level, Father?" pressed Quincy.

"Why *are* you here Quincy? Other than your interview answer you keep regurgitating back to me, you have never answered my question."

"My answer's not good enough?"

"Your answer is not truthful," he said.

"Why are *you* here, Father? asked Quincy, now slouched back deep in the sofa pillows, choking the armrest.

"I was inspired by Jean Vanier to lead this residence, and that's what I'm doing," he said, leaning forward on the edge of the sofa, his elbows on his knees.

"I'm here to be inspired by God to do good works," said Quincy.

"You are here because of a request. I agreed to that request," said Price.

"You agreed to the request because you had to agree to the request," said Quincy, now pushing herself up from the sofa pillows.

"You're still being untruthful Quincy. Anybody who is just slightly familiar with Personality Culture knows who you are, and knows what you are," he said, getting back up, with no intent to sit back down.

"How long have you had the Cynths here?" Quincy asked.

"A while."

"I ask you to power them down and let me do the kitchen work," said Quincy.

"Can't you work with them? They interact well teaming with humans."

"I'll bash them with a cook pot within the first ten minutes. And I know they're expensive," she said.

"Please. There's not enough to do around here. And you don't want me to start drinking your wines I know you have."

"We'll see," he said. Dealing with his mother had given Ash Price experience in dealing with Quincy. The women were different, but their inner core was identical, he thought, although mother was of the full batshit crazy variety. Quincy was at least a predictable, calculating, charmer of the first degree.

"Do you pray?" asked Father Price.

Quincy laughed.

"Do you read?"

"Not if I can help it," she said.

"If you are not living in delusion as a Catholic, then I find it a complete mystery as to why you do what you do—unless the equally mysterious Dr. Olivia Pernell I have heard about is aroused by your pretense," said Quincy.

"Where is Dr. Pernell, anyway? I was told she was on permanent staff here."

"Are you curious enough to want to learn to pray?" said Father Price.

Quincy rose from the sofa and thanked him for the conversation. It was exactly how she thought it would go, though disappointed she couldn't get a rise out of him. She figured the only way to continue to have any conversations with someone who could *actually* converse was to say 'yes' to his question--and she did. Although, she thought, she could have a conversation with Grace, and maybe, Jane. Quincy left Price's office feeling victorious; she was after all, always in it to win.

****

"Bullshit level--DEFCON 5! Take precautions!"

Quincy stopped at Petrol's door, which was ajar. Inside were Grace and Petrol doing a very poor job of trying to conceal high-pitched laughter. She knocked twice and then she heard, "Warning, warning! BULLSHIT ALERT!"

On the bed, between Grace and Petrol was a severely faded red plastic, desktop Bullshit Button. Petrol's room was full of light and stark as a monastery. Where Grace wore a suit every day, Petrol wore blue jeans and a red, round neck t-shirt. A different color t-shirt for every day of the week. Petrol knew enough--if someone was laughing then something was funny. Petrol laughed because Grace had the funniest laugh. Nothing gave him more pleasure than watching Curly Howard of the Three Stooges. If Petrol had more than a one hundred word vocabulary, he kept the other words to himself. If

Grace was not present, Petrol sat waiting, exactly like a dog for his master. Sometimes that was a burden for Grace.

Quincy assumed the BS button was their way of inviting her into their world, which was the first time they did so since she arrived. Did they perceive her as full of shit or a bullshit artist? Quincy assumed the latter--although they had spent almost no time together other than Mass and dinner. "Why are you here Quincy?" asked Grace, now standing, the level of effort reflected by his wince, and massaging his lower back.

"Thank you for asking. May I sit?" As Quincy pulled up the small desk chair and sat down, Petrol's hand inched towards the BS button.

"You are the only one who has asked me that, aside from Father Price during my interview, and again today."

"I'm here to pray for you, all the rest, and myself. And to do what needs to be done around here," said Quincy, pleased with her response and tone of conviction.

A piercing siren sounded--followed by, "BULLSHIT DETECTED! Take precautions!" Petrol handed the BS button over to Grace, who had motioned for it just after Petrol pushed the button.

Smiling, Quincy said, "Well, Petrol has spoken."

"Your hair is perfect, your makeup too. When you were less old, I'm certain you caused men to bumble about because they were severely distracted by your prettiness. Maybe they wrecked their cars."

"We see you do your yoga and tai chi in the courtyard in the early morning. You first arrived here in a Bentley."

"Out there in the world, you have everyone to mesmerize, yes? Here, you have such a small audience, and most with limited capacity to notice, or be mesmerized. I do not understand why you are here."

Quincy blanked out Grace's questions as if she were the one who experienced epileptic auras, and not Grace. She stood to face Grace and touched his shoulder. "Thank you for inviting me in." She then gave a small wave to Petrol, and he waved back, grinning.

"Good night," said Quincy.

Grace then helped Petrol get ready for bed.

"Petrol, brush your teeth, but not so hard. Your gums are not supposed to bleed." Grace then turned in for the night.

Quincy lay in bed but could not close her eyes. Doing so induced a creeping anxiety. But in staring at the ceiling fan in slow rotation she could at least imagine winning. Her first weeks at the Life Boat she stayed numb, thanks to her prescriptions. She let them run out. Alcohol withdrawal should not have kept her up at night, but yet she could not sleep, and unable to escape her thoughts of being insignificant. No children of her own gave her hours a day to persuade as many as conceivable that what she believed to be important was in fact all that was important to leading the right kind of life. And marrying a man of ridiculous wealth was much easier than she first imagined. Within the tight social circles and connecting circles of the ridiculously wealthy masters of charm existed at every stratum, each seeking every bit of self-righteous validation of their precious attributes they believed was inherently theirs to possess. Quincy regarded them as the most necessary people in the world, for they were to be competed against—it was a constant measuring of her personal attributes against theirs.

When Quincy had reached the top, she reveled in her victory for a time. Then, in an afternoon alone in her house so large disbelief in its enormity was the first impression, a sense of absurdity came lollygagging in--an out-of-the-blue realization that created a shock. Her swift emotional collapse led to doubt her immortality. Since content with total victory was living only on past successes, there was no other choice but to shut down—so said her therapist. And Quincy shut down. At sixty, the most courageous thing to do was to start from scratch, in an environment as unknown as she could possibly stand—so said her therapist, half-joking. Quincy went home and drank wine while lying in a thirty-two jet spray spa. That next day Quincy began the withdrawal away from the life she built. Only to prove again that any degree of joking with a narcissist is plain bad therapy and can have unpredictable and disruptive consequences—challenging the imagination.

Quincy needed to know she could rely on opportunities to winning over her competition, tomorrow, and the next day, and the next. That is why she wanted to believe this was the reason she was at the Life Boat. And Quincy stayed awake every night because she could not see any achievement that she could identify as a success. Her wine at least permitted her to dwell in the delusion that the past was also the future. With no wine at all, her senses knew better, which is why she continued to refrain from drinking. If Quincy had any realization at all of her motivations, she kept them so well hidden her therapist was convinced of her utter lack of self-awareness. But her therapist felt a professional obligation to hold out hope that Quincy was only phenomenal in her complete success at ignoring her self-awareness, not absent of complete knowledge of its existence. Quincy imagined that within the therapist's elite circle of psychiatrists around the world she was known as Patient Q. But they became inescapably aware of the influence of Stephen, who for them was the far greater mystery, far greater than why she walked away. Quincy tried to imagine she didn't mind the attention going to someone else.

****

On her knees knelt Quincy, pleading with Mary Osborne, yet pleased to be distracted by the Johnny Ramone poster behind her on the wall. A perfect Mosrite guitar stance, tall, lean, in leather and jeans, slashing barre chords with such a focus of passion, virtuosos had little choice but to give notice. Even Quincy had to agree.

"I'm a woman and I cannot help with the women here?"

"You are not a member," said Mary Osborne, confused as to why Quincy was in her room and on her knees.

"A member? Of the Life Boat? But I am!" said Quincy, in pain on the tile floor.

"Not of The Syndromes," said Mary Osborne, walking past Quincy to leave her room.

"I told you I know little about rock and roll, and I have never played any musical instrument," said Quincy, tired of thirty seconds on her knees, now getting up from the floor.

"Jane knows how to play guitar," said Mary Osborne, leaving her room.

"Why can't Jane play guitar for you?" asked Quincy.

"Jane has a penis. He showed it to me."

Quincy followed her out of the room, grabbing Mary Osborne's arm.

"Ok, Ok. I will go ask Jane to teach me to play guitar," said Quincy.

"Ok," said Mary Osborne.

"Ok," said Quincy.

Jane was the only one who approached Quincy soon upon her arrival. On two separate occasions he knocked on Quincy's door. The first time she ignored the knocks, unaware who was knocking, still pissed off being at the Life Boat. The second occasion Jane visited, Quincy asked who it was, and when Jane replied, Quincy said she wasn't feeling well and was turning in early. She convinced herself that Jane was a star struck fan of Celeb Culture and therefore, had to be ignored. Maybe it was the dress Jane was wearing. Quincy didn't care. She knew she didn't want any part of any conversation with Jane.

That evening, before Mary Osborne assisted the other women in getting ready for bed, Quincy knocked on Mary Osborne's door. Across the courtyard Jane stopped and looked up to watch Quincy talking with Mary Osborne, her door open enough only to see Mary Osborne's face. Jane noticed Quincy using her arms and hands while talking softly, with Mary Osborne statue still, listening. The conversation was not long. Mary Osborne closed her door and Quincy made her way to the dining room. Stepping inside, the motion sensor tuned the ceiling lighting to *soft evening glow.* She went to the kitchen, certain that at any moment White or Gray would motor out to meet her. She sat down by the window that faced the mountains, barely silhouette in the dusk.

"I'd like a glass of wine please," said Quincy, not hearing either Cynth but knowing they could hear her.

"Certainly Quincy," said Gray, now by her side.

"What type of wine would you prefer?" asked Gray.

"Surprise me," replied Quincy, feeling charged after her conversation with Mary Osborne.

"Ceremonial wine?" asked Gray. Quincy was watching Gray through the reflection off the window. *Funny,* thought Quincy.

"That *is* a surprise," she said, adding, "A Pinot Noir please."

"You have not asked for wine before, Quincy," said Gray.

"My own special Lenten Season," said Quincy.

"Lent has not arrived yet," said Gray.

"A Catholic Cynth no less!" said Quincy.

"Wine, please," she insisted.

"Certainly," replied Gray, gliding to the kitchen. The conversation with Mary Osborne had gone well, Quincy surmised. Gray returned with her Pinot Noir.

"Who taught you to pour?" asked Quincy, inspecting what little wine was in the glass.

"Normal pour, six ounces, Quincy," said Gray, posting like a guard next to her table. Quincy hadn't had a six-ounce glass of wine since she was eleven.

"There's a limit too, I bet, right?" said Quincy, tasting the wine, surprised it was a new bottle.

"Yes, two glasses," said Gray.

"Bring me one more please--and that will be all," she said.

"Certainly," said Gray. Quincy hated that reply from a waiter.

The Pinot Noir was good, and the glass was empty. Almost two months now, and the second glass will be even better, she thought. Drunk monks in monasteries responsible for the productivity advances in Europe, well, well, well. These were her first thoughts drinking alone, ever since her first lover said those words when he introduced her to beer. She'd grown up on wine. Beer was for fat women; her mother would say. Gray returned with the second glass and removed the empty one.

"Who drinks around here?" asked Quincy, feeling the first glass.

"Everyone drinks something," said Gray.

"I bet they do," she said, wanting to kick herself for talking to a damned Cynth.

"That is all, please leave now," she said.

"Certainly." If Quincy didn't leave now, Gray was not going to be in operating condition the next day.

Quincy got up and went outside, walking towards the chapel. She heard the low sound of far distant cars on the highway, and crickets close by. The sky was clear, as usual. Stars to Quincy were not a wonder to see, but an irritating reminder of the smallness of the world, which was her world, as she saw it. She approached the chapel entrance and stopped. She imagined sitting inside by herself, drinking her own wine, in the dark. She imagined herself praying, reciting all those prayers Catholics pray, over and over by rote, passing rosary beads between her fingers, while being distracted by anything but being in the chapel reciting prayers. Praying was as foreign a thought as she ever had, maybe more so. This was going to be an adventure. She finished her wine, leaving the empty glass on the nearest table next to the dining room entrance, and turned in for the evening.

Chapter 5

Today found Grace and Jane passing through the courtyard and walking towards the parking lot. A day to buy food and whatever else was needed at the Life Boat. It was the first time Petrol got to sit up front, and his excitement was evidenced by his fidgetiness repeatedly pulling out and releasing the seat belt.

Grace stopped in confusion. Jane stopped three steps later and turned around, wondering why Grace stopped. Through Petrol's lowered window Quincy leaned over and shouted, "Petrol demanded I take him with us today." She kissed Petrol on the cheek and he froze, letting his seat belt slap against his meager chest.

"I'm driving--get in--no thank you's are necessary. Petrol and I *are* going with you." This was not Mary Osborne's idea. But it gave birth to the idea Quincy was undertaking. She told Quincy to take the matter of learning to play guitar up with Jane himself.

"And...I have full blessing from Father Price— let's go!" lied Quincy.

"Petrol--don't sit there like a rock--next time I'll ask permission," she whispered, winking.

Jane slid open the side door and allowed Grace to enter first. She pulled out of the driveway and gunned the accelerator, excited and pleased at her escape, and capturing an audience. The sun shone hot and Quincy was thinking Grace might not be quite as comfortable out and about in his suit. She thought it must be summer weight and made of the latest synthetic blends that breathe in desert climes. She thought of Grace—and that thought pleased Quincy.

Since the spread of auto-drive routes and the subsequent steep tax to self-drive, the reduction of traffic congestion brought back very old memories that very few remembered. But self-drive was making a comeback in popularity and Quincy knew why. She hated the convenience of mindlessness of auto-drive.

"We have passed where we buy our food and things," said Grace, irritated, as he watched them drive by the food market. Jane frowned.

"We'll have all day to buy food. Right now, I'm taking us to the ocean. Be there in less than an hour and a half—promise," said Quincy.

"Grace," moaned Petrol, unlocking his seatbelt. Grace reached forward and lowered Petrol's seat to almost full recline, and Petrol maneuvered out of the front and into the back-bench seat to sit between Grace and Jane.

"Jane, would you care to sit up front with me?" asked Quincy.

"I'll stay here," said Jane. They exchanged glances through the rearview mirror. Jane managed a shy wave to Quincy.

"I'm going to need your help, Jane," said Quincy.

"As you know, in order for me to join the band I need to know how to play guitar. I don't own a guitar. I intend to buy one and I need your help with picking one out for me," said Quincy.

"Dago Bill's," said Jane.

"You sure?" said Quincy.

"Dago Bill's," said Jane.

"Will you be my navigator? Up here, in the front seat with me?"

"It's near the ocean," said Jane, now staring outside, his head resting on the window.

"You know Dago Bill?" asked Quincy.

"He's dead," said Jane.

"He's dead you say?"

"His daughter's alive," said Jane.

"Talk with her since you won't talk with me."

Good enough memory then, doesn't he, Jane the man? thought Quincy.

Grace calmed Petrol by holding his hand. But Grace had become angry, and his grip tightened. Quincy shifted her rear-view mirror to now see Petrol and Grace. Both looked forlorn, and Quincy was convinced Petrol's face mimicked Grace. She was wrong. Petrol's hand hurt like hell.

In her mind she called them the pathetic trio—definitely in need of a big meal. At the next stop light she did a U turn and three blocks later she pulled into The Rare Elements, possibly the best restaurant for heart arresting food of any kind, at any time. Twenty minutes later after finishing the famous grilled variety plate *En Total*, they were asleep. Quincy ate nothing, and her coffee was still almost too hot to drink. Traffic thickened during this stretch, but Quincy's mind was on getting them to the beach. They would lighten up and change their attitude, she predicted.

She made it to Cliffside Drive in about the time she expected. She stopped the van in front of the iron gate and rolled down the window. A red light prompted her to look into the small camera housed in the privacy wall. The light flashed green and the gate began to open. The three in the back were now coming awake as Quincy drove up the driveway and parked in front of a four door garage. In the semi-circular driveway were two pickup trucks used by the carpenters who were doing extensive work inside the main house.

"Wait here," she commanded. She left the van and went inside. A few minutes later she reappeared, motioning them to follow her into the garage. Grace gave the house and property a quick glance and followed Quincy, with Petrol following Grace. Jane stood by the side of the van and took in the view. He could see the ocean in between the garage and main house. Ignoring the others, Jane walked towards the ocean on a manicured path around the house. Below the small cliff was a thin strip of beach and small waves lapping up on the shore. Jane could hear men talking in a foreign language inside the main residence. The pounding sound of a hammer, then the unmistakable creak of long nails being removed by a claw. Jane's mind shut out the working carpenters and stared out at the ocean. He couldn't remember now but he used to stand and stare out at the water and horizon until his legs locked up, and then he would sit down and stare, until he was led away to where he lived. Returning from the garage Quincy now led Grace and Petrol back to the van, each with fishing poles and tackle box, and Quincy the same. After putting the fishing equipment in the back of the van, they joined Jane to stare at the ocean.

Sometime later, Grace said, "My family has a house on this street."

"Certainly not," said Quincy, surprised, then moments later not so surprised after all.

"I prefer the Life Boat," said Grace.

"I could live right here," said Jane, pointing to the ground beneath his feet.

"Here."

Petrol stared out in the distance. Grace lifted his hat and wiped his sweat.

"Jane, follow me," said Quincy nudging him, and she turned and walked to the van. The other two followed.

Other than the desalinization plant in view a half-mile offshore, the Malibu pier and its nearby surroundings remained unchanged since most locals thankfully could remember. The wounds from the desalinization battles were not imaginary; the four water riots killed 34 people. But the sweetness of victory was enduring with continuing evidence the great reduction in water prices was permanent. Fresh water scarcity was no longer leverage for the billionaires and their politicians. Quincy led them down the pier and let them see the fisherman leaning against the railing next to their poles, waiting for the signals fishermen teach themselves to observe, in hopes for a fish on the line. Quincy loved to fish from the pier. Since she was ten years old. She got it—why one fishes. Still, far more men, than women. She figured out why men fished. That is one reason why she loved men. She didn't care why women fished, she wanted to know why men did. Maybe women fished for the same reason men did. She found that answer unsatisfactory for what she believed to be all the obvious reasons. Quincy's only philosophical venture was to ask all the men fishing on the piers she fished, why they fished. Forty-five years of asking, less so nowadays. Knowing the answer was never as joyous as listening to their replies. Watching their faces— and eyes, as they attempted to answer the questions, reminded her of her father trying to answer the question.

"I have to." It was the best answer to the question because it was true—true with a capital T. Quincy found that to be the only truth with a capital T.

Petrol stopped to watch a fisherman reel in his line, his poled lowered as if paying homage to those creatures living in the ocean. He raced to the railing to witness the small mackerel being yanked from the water, wriggling in furious back and forth motions. Petrol was mesmerized by the deliberate ascension of the mackerel towards the fisherman, already judging the length of the fish too small to keep. With speed, the fisherman grabbed the mackerel, and with pliers in the other hand, dislodged the hook in a firm, but tender motion, letting the mackerel slip from his hands down to the water. The splash upon the surface covered the mackerel's deep charge to safety.

"We'll be making this trip a regular event I can see already," said Quincy aloud, in full self-approval. She knew Jane would be content just standing on the pier looking out. But Grace, she was not so sure.

"I fish off this pier," said Quincy.

"Grace, tell me you like to fish."

"You don't seem like a fisherman," said Grace, not failing to notice how excited Petrol was watching the fishermen.

"Love it. I dress like a man and spend half the day pier fishing. I hate boats."

"Why do you fish? To dress like a man, like Jane dresses like a woman?"

"I have come to believe it's the solitude I prefer, given a choice."

"You have a choice?"

"Of course, I have a choice."

"Lucky."

"It's easier to fish dressed like a man."

Grace looked at Quincy. He smiled the kind of smile when he was entering an epileptic aura. After a lifetime, he knew his symptoms well. Confused euphoria--that was how he described the feeling. Most times it was the time of day, nothing else. Or maybe thought Grace, it was being on Cliffside Drive again. He sat down on the boardwalk planks and waited until the next stage. He smiled, thinking maybe

48

he wasn't destined to be a fisherman. Then the convulsions came. Flopping like a fish on a pier.

Grace was late to insert his mouthpiece, so Petrol rushed to his side, withdrew it from Grace's suit coat pocket, and firmly inserted the mouthpiece between Grace's teeth, wrapping the attached band around his head. Petrol lifted Grace's head and rested it in his lap. He leaned over to retrieve Grace's fedora, putting it on his own head for safekeeping.

Jane's long skirt lifted in the unexpected breeze. He was wearing pink boxer shorts underneath. He signaled Petrol a thumb's up--as a question. Petrol replied with a confidant thumb. Jane nodded, and returned to staring towards the horizon, making a note of seagulls just above him eyeing with envy the progress of the fishermen. Soon after, the seizure subsided, and Grace rested in the lap of Petrol.

Watching Quincy observe the seizure was a man, thin, with full white hair tossed about, and reeling in his line. His age was indeterminate. But he stood tall, inspecting the liveliness of his bait, while watching Quincy through his sunglasses. He set down his fishing pole and pushed his hair back, put on a short brimmed straw hat that he had clipped to his belt. He tipped his hat upon Quincy noticing him.

Now Grace was awake amidst fishermen and pier visitors who began to circle him. He got up quickly, a bit too quick, bent over to relieve the sudden head rush, then arose again and brushed himself off. Through his mouthpiece he smiled and whispered a garbled thanks to Petrol and removed his hat from Petrol's head and placed it upon his own. Jane parted the crowd with a gentle movement of his arms and soon everyone was about their business on the pier. Except for the white haired man wearing the straw hat, no one paid attention to Quincy's own seizure of total helplessness. She stood as marble. She had never engaged in the drama of other's lives, there was no concern; therefore, there was no need. But her husband changed everything. She at first pretended that was not so. Then unable to keep pretending, she buried a second big Truth about her husband. She would say to him expect little from her—just regular sex and an impressive instinct for the weaknesses of his competitors. But Stephen knew Quincy knew. Stephen was the shock to Quincy's being.

What happened on the pier today, for some reason, was a reminder of the shock of Stephen.

Quincy changed her mind. Much to Jane's disappointment, they didn't stop at Dago Bill's music store.

Before returning to the Life Boat, they pulled into the food market. Grace remained asleep in the van while the rest went shopping. Petrol's job was to tick each item off the grocery list. He loved this job. Quincy pointed to what item needed ticking off and with great pride, Petrol made a check mark by each item.

Chapter 6

If not for the rapid knock on the door, Quincy would have slept on through the morning. Never had she stayed asleep so long, even on her late, late party nights. She put on her robe and peeked through the small opening of her door, only bright sunlight greeting her. She listened for a second and heard nothing. Returning her robe to the closet, she noticed the fishing poles leaning in the back corner. Her memory of Grace in a seizure on the pier included the tall white haired man. His thick hair was brilliant white. She was trying to remember his face. What kind of smile was it? The puzzle of his smile stayed with her. It was already too hot for coffee but Quincy didn't care. This morning she was ready for two cups.

Even though breakfast had long been served, everyone remained in the dining room. The new face had to be Dr. Olivia Pernell, Quincy thought, noticing the fond reaction to her return. *She was one of those*, thought Quincy. One of those women who required little effort or self-attention to look beautiful. Conversation lessened as Olivia stood to greet Quincy. In the six steps until they formerly greeted one another with a handshake (for they already greeted each other with glances as soon as Quincy entered the dining room) Quincy noticed everything about Olivia; the flow of her light dress on her slender physique, her legs fit for a runway but without the catwalk sway, the v-neckline low enough to invite a notice, a remarkable neck for a women maybe a few years younger than Quincy, light wrinkles only in the eyes, no makeup necessary because of her fine features, and pulled back, very light brown hair concealing very well the slow invasion of gray. She was haute monde, a personage with ability or training to assimilate into any group--that gift unrecognizable, thought Quincy--to most of the world who don't notice.

"Quincy." She held out her hand and smiled as if she was charmed at first sight. A smile perfected.

"Olivia." She accepted her hand with a slight hesitation, but then gave a firm shake in return. In part, because she was a psychiatrist, Dr. Pernell conducted her own assessment in between the six steps until their handshake. The difference was Olivia long ago stopped caring about what Quincy lived for. But an irritation arose upon their greeting, and Olivia was not pleased with herself.

"An eventful day yesterday, from what I hear," said Olivia smiling--hers of the more professional kind.

Her tone and even-metered delivery was like that of Quincy's psychiatrist, and after most sessions Quincy wanted to strangle her therapist because of it. The other times she wanted to strangle her therapist was because she viewed psychiatry as a borderline criminal enterprise. At least for the haute monde, Quincy thought, smiling to herself—therapy must work because otherwise her lack of restraint would result in a strangled doctor of the mind.

Like Olivia, Quincy became aware of everyone else gathered.

"Oh yes," said Quincy, now looking over to Grace, asking, "Feeling better today?"

He smiled and nodded, and gave a glance to Father Price, who, never thinking about what the meeting between Olivia and Quincy would be like, never a thought in the world about their first encounter, returned Grace's smile, accompanied with a wide-eyed expression of belated, amusing surprise.

"I understand you have been on a journey of some sort. Is that right?" asked Quincy.
Addressing her as Doctor was out of the question.

"You can call it that," said Dr. Pernell.

"Starting tomorrow there will be new residents arriving. We are going to be busy!"

"You arrived last night then?"

"Yes. And you are from?" asked Olivia.

54

"Oh, not far from here actually."
"And you love to fish I take it."
"Oh, I do. I do," beamed Quincy.
Jane watched and thought--no catfight?

Chapter 7

The bent man was the first arrival of Olivia Pernell's new group. He came with an old steel grocery cart that he could not be without. Stooped over its worn-off, red plastic handle the bent man was at peace once in touch with his wobble wheeled chariot. Olivia could only guess how long he had been on the streets. When he did speak it was an inaudible whisper, in part because his beard covered his mouth. He motioned with his head and communicated through his eyes, either way you had to bend below him to come into eye contact, for he always appeared as if he was picking something up from the ground.

The first thoughts of Quincy were to get his wheels replaced since Olivia informed her that he could not be separated from that particular grocery cart. The sound of the wobble of those tired wheels, well past their service life being pushed along the sidewalks and streets of every condition, was intolerable. He had no connections to anyone, no name he was willing to divulge, and no willingness to remain within the confines of anyplace, including the Life Boat. Perhaps he knew enough to know that his days on his own were over. He was too feeble to continue living the street way, no matter the regularity in which he was fed, clothed, and bathed and shaved by the charities that administered to the streets. The charity people called him Cart. Like a temperamental dog, he sometimes responded to the name. That's how the charity lady described him when Olivia entered his life. Cart was maybe local, or not. His complexion was a furrow of bad skin wrinkles, wild eyebrows, and full and knotted grey hair so brittle it broke when attempted to be brushed. It appeared dirt was imbedded in his pores. But Cart could eat and drink of his own ability, hold a cup, hold a fork, cut with a knife. After ensuring they recovered everything from the pockets of Cart's shirt, pants, jacket and coat, Grace and Petrol, along with Jane, burned his clothes, without approval. Flames leaped high from the accumulated grease of his living. He seemed to have accumulated nothing else--his cart was empty. If he collected anything he either used it or gave it away. No one knew which. Father Price never knew about the burning, spending more time away from the Life Boat due to pressing needs for priests within the region. This is what he told everyone.

Throughout the week new residents arrived. All women. They were from separate homes where their families were their caretakers and they no longer were going to take care of them anymore. Legally all the women met the criteria to be euthanized. They qualified to die at the time of the families choosing. Olivia chose the women and negotiated the terms of accepting them as residents of the Life Boat. Two of the families declined to contribute but the other family more than made up for the other two. It was crucial to have the funding source, not only to cover the expenses of the Life Boat, but as insurance against any interference from the state.

These new residents were in their twenties and thirties, with severe mental limitations. Quincy and Olivia had little choice but to work together. Adding Cart was a last minute decision.

It was the charity woman's victory--Marjorie Bentham--to get one of hers into the Life Boat. Olivia knew her. Mrs. Bentham was a former church lady the likes of which old comedians used as part of their routine. There was no surprise that St. Paul the Apostle was her personal hero. Ten years she worked with the forgotten on the streets. Mrs. Bentham made it clear to Olivia she very much desired to be an assistant at the Life Boat, as long as she became director and separated from the Catholic Church. On her own authority, Marjorie Bentham knew better than ever to trust the Church again, on any matters, and so took it upon herself to proselytize as a true acolyte of St. Paul's, whom she swore had visited her in a vision and told her to follow a different path of the Church, since its corruption was complete. She was in search for a new mission.

The Life Boat was now full. All the rooms were occupied. After the residents were in their rooms for the evening, Quincy lay across her bed, exhausted as she never had been. She had no experience of exhaustion, physical or otherwise. Her life was magical, as almost everyone never experienced or imagined. She lay there, cursing in whispers. If not for her rage keeping her awake, she would have been asleep in an instant. Keeping her commitment to not having alcohol in her room was well beyond a stupid decision, almost as stupid as the decision to come to the Life Boat. She pulled herself up from her bed and opened her door, taking in the view of the courtyard and noticing a light on in the dining room. Quincy disapproved of her look in the mirror, combing her hair with her eyes closed, and after, made her way to the dining room where she found Olivia sitting and having tea. In the past week they had received all of the new women residents and as each arrived the more overwhelmed Quincy became.

"I'll join you if you don't mind, after I make a stop in the kitchen," said Quincy.

Olivia looked up above her reading glasses and offered a small smile. In the kitchen, White and Gray were idle as coat racks in a desert summer afternoon until their motion sensors detected Quincy.

"Stay put, both of you," Quincy commanded. Neither moved as she retrieved a bottle of white wine from the refrigerator and uncorked it. With the bottle and a glass from the cupboard, she joined Olivia at the table. Quincy poured a full glass of wine and two sips later she topped off her glass.

"How many times have you had second thoughts since you arrived?" asked Olivia, taking off her glasses and placing them on her portable computer. Quincy sipped her wine. To date she had not known that Olivia drank, if she did, thought Quincy, she would call out White or Gray to fetch a bottle for her.

"Oh, as often as you probably imagined."

"I thought you just as soon leave the Life Boat than sit with me and talk," said Olivia, finishing her tea.

"I've never seen you drink," said Quincy.

"I prefer Scotch."

"White and Gray!" called out Quincy. Gray motored out with a bottle and a glass.
In front of Olivia, Gray poured her a small Scotch.

"Their voice detection range still amazes me, and pisses me off," said Quincy.

"Where did you all get those two?"

"Early prototypes. A gift."

"I have no reason not to talk to you Olivia."

Olivia said, "You have been very cooperative in taking instructions in how to care of our residents. I've been intending to tell you. I thank you for this."

"You have been thanking me all the time Olivia. You can stop now," said Quincy, noting her bottle was two thirds empty. She was the opposite of Olivia, her glass in no need of refill.

"And Father Price, he is where?" said Quincy, refilling her glass.

"He returns late tonight."

"From where?"

"He makes a circuit around the communities in this area that still desire to have a priest. God is making somewhat of a comeback." Olivia re-offered her small smile, as if offering any more would incur a deep personal loss. Olivia spoke as if also exhausted, but Quincy was not certain.

All the questions Quincy had held back from asking Grace and Jane about both Ash Price and Olivia were going to be asked to Olivia--when Quincy believed Olivia might actually answer.

Quincy said, "We have quite a few women here now. I don't count Jane. He's a man and that's that. Taking care of them all—just you and me—is not going to end well. They'll run us into the ground. We need more women assistants. God damn it, I'm even praying for them to arrive. And I never pray."

"It's a community we are building here, a small community to live amongst those that appear to have very little capacity to do anything or be anyone. They are not able to be anyone beyond themselves. They barely possess a self. What little they do possess, we must find it for them. And then give it back to them."

"What possibly could it be that they possess Olivia?" Her bottle empty, Quincy was now drunk, thanking the Lord Jesus.

"Oh, don't tell me, don't tell me..." said Quincy, eyeing Olivia's bottle of Scotch, knowing Scotch would obliterate her.

"Don't tell me..."

Olivia finished her drink, waiting to refill it after Quincy attempted to answer her own question. Olivia was not drunk--she liked Quincy.

Quincy blurted, "Love! God's love!" She broke out in laughter.

"What does that even mean? God's love?" said Quincy. The response surprised Olivia, and merited one more small Scotch, also pouring an equal measure into Quincy' wine glass.

"Yes, I believe you're right about love. However, I certainly am not the one to know what God's love means. Ash can try to explain for you." Quincy leaned toward Olivia and whispered, she did not want those two fucking robots to hear anymore of her conversation.

"Try? You are telling me you don't believe in God?" Quincy downed her Scotch like a shot.

"I believe love does exist," said Olivia, taking her first sip of her second drink.

"But I asked you about God."

"I believe love does exist, even in our residents."

"But I asked you about God."

"I know what you asked."

"And?" Quincy was lying on the table, too tired to sit in her chair.

"And nothing, other than what I've said," replied Olivia. In silence they stared at each other. Then Olivia finished her drink and lifted Quincy up. Arm in arm, Olivia walked with Quincy. Quincy recovered once she started walking. She let go of Olivia, said goodnight, and made her way back to her room.

Chapter 8

In attending to the residents, the evening gathering was a division of tasks disguised as dinner. Gurgling and grunts substituted for extended conversation. Quincy, Olivia, Father Ash, along with Grace, fed the residents by hand. Mary Osborne took care of her band mates, only with the help of Jane. Cart ate bent over, with his dinner in the top foldout section of his grocery cart. He had permitted Jane to trim his mustache off his lips. The assistants ate while feeding the residents. By the sixth dinner, the new arrivals stopped moaning about missing their families, if that was the reason for their moaning. At the end of dinner, all the dishes were loaded into Cart's cart and taken into the kitchen.

While Olivia was successful in bringing residents to the Life Boat, Father Price knew he was a failure in bringing the faithful to assist in their living. Olivia would not believe in God, Quincy believed God was not worth believing in. Jane refused to talk about faith. Petrol was a mimic and Mary Osborne was a rock and roller. If the women residents possessed a capacity for faith it would remain unknown to anyone but them. Only Grace was a Catholic. And Cart? He only talked with Jane, and Jane refused to talk about what they talked about.

That evening, at Mary Osborne's insistence, everyone gathered on the second floor. The heat seeped away, and the cool air brought calmness to them all. In the distance, acetylene welders affixing connections along the VacTrain line punctuated the surrounding working lights. The bright plumes are what Mary Osborne watched for every night.

Every night was almost as important as the following night she said, because soon the inauguration of the VacTrain line was to be held. This news is what Grace told Jane, who told Mary Osborne. As much as Mary Osborne wanted to be a rock and roll bass player she also wanted to be far away in a near instant. This she could imagine.

"And maybe back again and maybe not," she told Jane. The line connected the north with the south—seven hundred miles, at seven hundred miles per hour. The women residents were unaware of VacTrains traveling in a near instant, yet they too wanted to be elsewhere—perhaps the comfort of their bed with music in their ears. Grace thought so. They either loved Mozart or loved electronic dreamy pieces, heavy on repetitive, melody lines that inspired yearning. No one liked banjos or Dvorak, especially Symphony Number Nine. Grace said the fact they all loved music was a note from God. Grace thought if they listened to Number Nine while on the VacTrain they might change what little mind they possessed. Grace seemed certain about this.

Father Price was in equal fascination with the completion of the VacTrain line. In his mind he was lost in a distant setting. Olivia saw starlight reflection in his watered eyes and knew it was time. She smiled alone.

Quincy was lost in the change of being an assistant at the Life Boat; its pace, priorities, and privations. But her being lost felt more as freedom and did not translate into sorrow. In that realization, she almost smiled because she felt she was tip toeing on top of a quiet, deep lake of melancholy, ever confidant she wouldn't sink.

She wanted to go fishing, and this time she was bringing Father Price as a test of her buoyancy--and maybe his, for he was unable to hide the burden he shouldered, only its content.

Chapter 9

Sunday Mass at the chapel. For reasons Father Price would never know, attendees stood in the back, not family members but others with no affiliation to the Life Boat. During his directorship, he would never see a congregation of this size. Father Price's delivery reflected he was not pleased. His tone and abruptness undermined his homily on humility. He was not pleased because the night before he accepted Quincy's invitation to go fishing--with no resistance. He was unable to resist without appearing as a complete sanctimonious, self-occupied fool, much like he perceived Quincy to be. And now he was helping her load the van with fishing equipment and sundries for the outing. No Mass with the outlying communities today. The morning was hot and near cloudless. For Father Price, the lure of the pier was the cool ocean breeze.

Quincy told Grace part of the truth. She was taking Father fishing to convince him that it could be a regular activity for the residents. Through Grace, Quincy mollified both Petrol and Jane. Grace was still unsure; his last seizure was while fishing. But he loved the feeling of being extended out over the ocean, if only for the length of the pier.

Before starting the van, Quincy turned to Price and said, "I figure you to be someone who feels the need to be in control so I'll say this: we are going to the Malibu pier and fish. I've fished there for years and it is where I brought Grace, Petrol, and Jane. I have all the equipment and know what I'm doing. The residents need outlets and this can be one of them. I'll bait your hook and tell you where to cast. You'll know when a fish is on. I assume, of course, you never fished before. Am I right?"

"Of course I'm right," she replied, noting Price nodding in the affirmative. He drew a breath through his nose and held it, strapped on his seat belt and said, "What are we trying to catch?"

"Mackerel."

"With?"

"With grocery store shrimp."

"Why mackerel?"

"They fight like hell."

"Don't we require fishing licenses?"

"Not on public piers. We go to my spot and start fishing."

"And you enjoy this?"

"I love it."

"Why are you at the Life Boat, Quincy?"

"Why are you, Father?"

They road in silence for the next half hour. The traffic was light. Then Quincy pulled into a store.

"Coming?" she asked.

They exited the van and went in to get shrimp, ice, some sandwiches, water and wine. Back in the van she uncorked the Sauvignon Blanc and filled two metal, insulated bottles she brought with her.

Ash poured the ice into the coolers and got back in the van.

"We'll be there in ten minutes," said Quincy.

"I usually have a small wagon that I load up but you'll have to take the coolers and I'll handle the rest," she said.

On the pier the temperature was pleasant and the breeze whirled around them. She pointed to a spot on the left side of the pier. Quincy wasted no time organizing their spot, baiting the hooks, and demonstrating how to cast. She handed the rod to Price and he reeled in the line and listened while Quincy stepped him through once more how to cast.

"Nice cast," she said. Quincy cast out just left and inside where Price's line entered the water. It was a spectacular morning with excellent visibility. A day that exemplified why so many who visited never wanted leave.

"You know I'm here at Olivia's request, or shall I say insistence," said Price.

"Sure," said Quincy, now concentrating on her line in the water.

"And you thought we wouldn't get along, didn't you?"

"She is the most resilient and adaptive woman I know," he said aloud, adding, "Or will ever know," under his breath. It was no effort for Quincy to convert his reply into a personal compliment. A compliment almost always was present in any reply to her, she thought, whether said aloud or indicated in expression. It was her first reflex to think so, ever since she could remember.

"She is strong and seemingly most capable of anything. And she is attractive," said Quincy, not needing to read his expression.

Price's pole dipped down and with little hesitation he jerked, with more pull than necessary. Out of water popped his leader and hook, with no fish. He reeled in the line to replace the bait. Quincy said nothing, concentrating instead on her line. As Price cast out, Quincy announced, "Fish on." Her pole bent as she set the hook with a small quick jerk. She waited a moment to confirm she hooked the fish and then began reeling in. A lightweight pole and four pound test line made for a sporty catch. As the mackerel broke the surface she estimated no more than ten inches, eleven tops. Maybe a few residents will have fresh fish tonight, she thought, as she removed the hook and settled the still fighting mackerel on top of the ice. With the lid shut, the fish could be heard thrashing about.

"Nice catch," said Price. Quincy smiled and thanked him, placed a shrimp upon her hook and cast out. She was unsure if Price was enjoying himself. Maybe it was because he was with her or, fishing wasn't to his liking. Perhaps the less said between them the better.

This is exactly what Ash Price was thinking. The less they spoke the more he could focus on fishing off a pier on a beautiful day. Without thinking about much of anything, almost an impossible task for him. Such was his habit. The essence of his preoccupation was now well known to him, thanks to Olivia. Being outdoors gave him relief from preoccupation.

Quincy took a gulp of wine.

"I know you won the lottery years ago, back in Baltimore," announced Quincy.

Price remembered the wine. He picked up the insulated bottle and took a sip, and then another.

"You won millions, then disappeared, she said, adding, "Even my Ex's number one man, Victor, couldn't trace you until you took over the Life Boat. That's quite an accomplishment."

"My only," he quipped.

Price's poled dipped. This time he waited until he felt another tug. He set the hook like Quincy did. Successful this time, Price reeled in the mackerel, about the same length as Quincy's. As he brought the mackerel onto the pier, Quincy placed her pole in the holder attached to the railing and opened her tackle box.

"Gut hooked," she said, reaching for the line. She grabbed the mackerel and without hesitation inserted the long-nose pliers into the fish, wincing as she pulled the hook out from its gut. She placed the fish in the cooler, baited his hook and motioned for Price to cast out, which he did.

"Thank you," he said.

"Gut hook is something you deal with and avoid if you can," she said.

"Something to hide?" said Quincy.

"Feel of the bite and quick hook setting," she said, taking another drink of wine, "That's all I can tell you."

"Good advice," said an unknown voice behind her.

Although startled, Quincy turned and recognized him in an instant. The tall man at the pier, when Grace had his seizure. He was dressed the same, but now his presence was intimate.

"Mr. Galvin Salvus," he said. His accent was untraceable. Perhaps no accent at all, she thought, just one she thought she heard, or wanted to hear.

"I have fish guts on my hands," she said. She held her hand out and he clasped her hand in a firm shake. Firm but not too, she thought.

"Quincy," she announced.

"Father Ash Price," she said, nodding to Price. He held up his hand to show it was clean and shook Galvin's hand. Mr. Salvus slipped him a business card.

"I'm off to the end of the pier, to my favorite spot," said Mr. Salvus, picking back up his tackle box.

"Good fishing to you both."

As Mr. Salvus walked on, Price read the card.

"What does it say?" asked Quincy.

"Applying for Life Boat residency. Includes his name and number."

"What!" she asked.

"That's it," lied Ash. The card also said, "I have the same referral as Quincy." It included a second phone number.

Price slipped the card in his pocket. They sipped their wine and fished, saying nothing to each other. Until Quincy's questions, Price found himself surprised to be relaxed, almost without rumination. Quincy was almost as intrigued by Mr. Galvin Salvus as she was about Price's past. She swore to herself she just wanted to fish, but she was going to find out about Price.

Father Price's new preoccupation ceased when he realized the undulation of the pier was not wine going to his head on a beautiful sunny day. Looking past Quincy, fixating on the end of the pier, he noted a mix of concern and confusion amongst the fisherman and visitors. Then a few began reeling in their lines very fast. Some now grabbed their gear and began to run. Price pushed Quincy to move.

"Let's go now, Quincy--right now." Startled out of her wine trance, she looked about, still unsure what was happening. He handed his fishing pole to Quincy, grabbed the two coolers and motioned for Quincy to move.

"Run!" shouted Price. The undulation grew severe. Everyone was running from the pier. Now at the van, both of them winded, the ground still moving beneath them, Price dropped the coolers and bent over, hands on his knees, his lungs demanding air. Quincy opened the sliding door and placed the poles inside the van. As she reached for the coolers Price blocked her hands. He put them in the van himself. The ground tremble stopped.

"No sense going anywhere right now," he said.

"I had no intention of going anywhere," said Quincy, climbing into the driver's seat.

Some cars were leaving the parking lot in panic, but many stayed put. Everyone was tuning into a radio station or on their PEDs trying to find news of the earthquake. A considerable aftershock rumbled her van.

Quincy thought about Mr. Salvus, and while searching for him and not seeing him, thought of the Life Boat in abstract, in what it represented, not the inhabitants themselves. Price's thoughts were on Olivia, as always, and too of the residents. He knew Jane would be of great help to Olivia at this moment and prayed Grace would not succumb to a seizure. Quincy's thoughts settled on Price.

"You're not going to say anything to me? Where've you been in between winning the lottery and running the Life Boat?"

Price was slightly drunk, alert enough to drive, but not judicious enough to stay silent.

Finally, he answered, "Trying to save some of humanity, one cause at a time."

"That's why Olivia Pernell fell for you...," Quincy wondered aloud. "An idealist supreme."

"I have a rotten success rate so far. Look at the Life Boat. Just barely above pathetic."

Quincy's tone changed.

"Maybe you're not the saving humanity type." She thought to herself, maybe he's the type who falls in love with being the hero—and why not? The priest with millions and the beautiful, intelligent Olivia

Pernell to help make it so. Quincy wondered, maybe all to impress her? Maybe they feed each other's infatuations? Hopscotching about--committed to a fantasy of godliness and sacrifice?

"Maybe," said Price, trying to place a phone call.

Neither Price nor Quincy could reach anyone by PED. Then another aftershock. Unable to drive anywhere because of the roads and highways being shut down, Father Price left the van to see if he could be of any assistance to anyone. Quincy stayed put and finish drinking her wine. She muttered something disquieting, addressed to Stephen her Ex, got out of the van, and followed Price back to the pier. It remained a beautiful sunny day.

The pier was empty but the two restaurants remained open, a testament to the latest construction advances in earthquake zones. At the pier, no one was injured. Everyone was waiting for further news of the extent of the damage. The epicenter was assessed to be north and well inland, but traffic was slow going along the coast, and east and west bound. Quincy noticed everyone was talking on their PEDs, while just previously, no one could. But she and Price failed to reach any one at the Life Boat. Soon Price was answering phone calls and messages from families whose daughters were residents. They too were unable to reach anyone at the Life Boat, and yet none of them offered to go to the Life Boat and check on their daughter. The two other priests Father Price knew within a few hours drive were busy in their own communities.

Quincy allowed herself this one exception. She called and left a message for Stephen. She thought about whether Stephen would have called first. He would have, she told herself.

It was 9 pm when Price and Quincy pulled into the Life Boat parking lot. Six hours to get back. The most severe damage was north and east.

Mt. San Antonio appeared unfazed by the quake, observed Quincy, before darkness came. Power was either never shut down or restored early on in their surrounding area. Though dark, no apparent damage was noticed as she and Price walked quickly through to the dining area and kitchen. There were no lights on in any of the rooms upstairs, not at all unusual given that everyone went to bed early. Father Price placed the coolers in the kitchen. Quincy called out to him from the dining area.

They split up to look for anyone. Quincy checked the resident's rooms, opening their doors slowly, so as not to awaken them, as if they were in their beds asleep. They all were asleep. But Grace, Petrol, James, Mary Osborne, and Cart were not in their rooms.

Chapter 10

Galvin Salvus knew everything about the world, but in the mirror, he had no recognition of himself. He saw an ancient man, but not himself; not how he appeared in the beginning. Salvus could only guess why he appeared so—perhaps so that the verities of time could be annotated.

He was to find Quincy and have her believe in what he had to say. He knew most would believe what was told to them, and many would believe the most extreme and severe of what they were told. Rare were those who would not believe because they would not be deceived. Quincy was singular--but not rare. But he was unsure about her. And his uncertainty was foreign to him, but far less so than his collection of worries.

Salvus was to remain with Quincy. There was no 'until'. He was to remain with Quincy, regardless whether she believed or not. It did not escape his notice he found her on the pier, amongst those fishing. So much of himself was no longer reachable, only the awareness of being aware of being something different. Physical pain was also as foreign--it was unexpected. Despair was so foreign it frightened him to think of it. Anger felt familiar as his skin, as did pride. But nothing was more frightening than the sudden onslaught of complete remembrance of humility, as if it was never known, and the belief of being unable to achieve it. Now that Salvus had made a connection with Quincy, he thought of many things at once. It was dizzying. His awareness of feelings was disconcerting. All this affected him as dreadful lead weights hooked to his body. Although a thin man with little to hook onto, he was laden down. He was heavy. It bent him.

Galvin Salvus knew everything about the world. Immersed in it, he now only believed he was a mere speck of dust.

Chapter 11

Price joined Quincy in the dining area.

"The chapel," he said, and she followed him. Other than six hours driving to go such a short distance, he had forgotten about the earthquake. Outside the air was cool and dry. The stars seemed brighter than normal.

Opening the chapel door, Father Price said, "Mr. Salvus wants to apply to be an assistant, and left his phone number."

"You don't know him at all?" he asked.

Quincy stopped short of entering the chapel.

"I saw him on the pier when I took them fishing. He stopped for a moment, looked at us helping Grace, and then walked on."

"That's it?"

"Why are you asking?" she said.

"Father!" Petrol yelled and ran to him. Father Price accepted Petrol's tight embrace, still thinking of Olivia.

Irritated, Quincy entered the chapel and looking past Father Price and Petrol, took note of who was present, noting Olivia's absence.

Father Price and Petrol walked together down the center aisle. Quincy elected to walk down the right aisle, where Grace, Jane and Mary Osborne sat. They all stood.

As Quincy walked, she thought about what she wanted to say and ask of them all. She knew Price had only Olivia on his mind, like Quincy now had Stephen.

Everyone began talking at once, except Jane and Cart. About when they felt the earthquake, how long it might last, the inability to reach anyone for help. None of the residents were aware of what was happening, as the first quake was felt as dinner was finished. They had an unexpected guest for dinner, they said. It was Marjorie Bentham. She had come to see Olivia. After getting the residents settled in for the evening, Olivia and the Bentham woman went into Father Price's office.

One by one they stopped talking over one another. Then Grace finished telling their story.

"Dr. Pernell told us she had to go with the Bentham woman for some emergency and to tell you she will return soon. She packed a small bag and then left with that lady. A note is on your desk."

Jane announced, "Cart knows the Bentham woman—from the streets."

Cart spoke up for the first time, surprising everyone. "She's the fervent type--jam packed with zeal. A lot of us are off the streets these days. Better places to live now that the do-gooders put their money where their mouth is. So, what's a woman like Bentham going to do? She's a real fervent type, I tell you."

"You take me fishing next time?" asked Cart.

"You smell the fish on me?" said Quincy.

"I'd like to go fishing sometime," said Cart.

"Then we'll go fishing," said Quincy.

Marjorie Bentham brought him to the Life Boat. Cart wasn't sure why she chose him, and why she chose the Life Boat. He didn't know what she thought of him, but he made sure she knew her attention was appreciated, even though he cared little for her. But Cart liked Quincy right away.

Quincy found it remarkable she had not craved for an exfoliation, pulsing shower, and clean clothes— until now. She was sticky with mackerel scent. She looked at Cart—how many showers did he miss in one year on the street?

Quincy leaned closer and asked, "What's wrong with your back?"

"Bent Over-itis."

She liked Cart.

Quincy was a keen observer, in possession of a foundational instinct she used to detect and exploit the fickleness of the human condition, and fiercely adept at delusion in service to her ego, which was as

82

tall and fragile as a grand ballroom glass chandelier. She knew Cart liked her too.

Father Price went to his office to read Olivia's note. Everyone else left to go to bed. Quincy followed Price. She found him leaning back in his desk chair, the note opened on the desk.

"What does Olivia's note say?"

"She's gone for more than a short while. She's now returning to Thailand because she feels she is urgently needed there."

"In Thailand? Why Thailand?"

"I met Olivia there. She was a director of an orphanage for children that were rescued from sex traffickers. They need her help."

"And this Bentham woman, she knows Olivia well?"

"I don't believe so."

"Isn't Thailand a dangerous place these days?"

"Very," he said.

Chapter 12

Quincy's first instinct was--naturally--to go straight to her bathroom and not emerge until fully satisfied she had removed all traces of anything other than what she was accustomed. She lay in her bed, anticipating aftershocks, and thinking through the scenarios that could play out for her with Olivia absent. Her Life Boat experience was not to be another game in which she could have her fun. Therapy was a game for Quincy. Her therapist appeared to be entirely sincere and dedicated to helping her gain some sense of sensitivity towards others, besides Stephen. Or something like that, she thought--imagine spending your time talking to people and believing you were helping them somehow, to make better choices in life, or stop behaving in a certain way--or her favorite, to help someone cope with some pick-an-anxiety. What complete shit, she thought. Petrol ought to be banging away on his BS button for sure. When she tired of that game, she stopped going to therapy. There was no winning or losing, just talking about feelings.

The Life Boat was not supposed to be a game. She came here because of her Ex, who put a challenge to her in such a way she had to accept. It was an outrageous challenge and she accepted without a thought in her mind about what going to the Life Boat would be like. She had no idea why Stephen proposed the challenge. She never asked at the time. And now it seemed to matter less and less why. She missed him. One day maybe, she thought, she would leave a message on his phone and tell him. But not today. She finally fell asleep in the remaining dark hours of the morning, and awoke in later morning, breathless and startled from her dream.

The break from the heat was noticeable; the gray high clouds blocked the sun, teasing, as if the clouds were actually going to produce rain. Aside from an intermittent, terse breeze that bent the courtyard grass, the Life Boat was still. Gray and White were back in action, delivering to the table trays of food. There were scrambled eggs, a mound of bacon, fried potatoes, doughnuts, and toast and jam.

All the residents were seated; Jane and Mary Osborne were standing, along with Grace and Petrol. Absent was Father Price. Petrol waved and smiled at Quincy. The celebratory mood was contagious to the women residents seated at the table.

Quincy's skeptical glance prompted Grace to add, "The earthquake hit some areas north very hard."

Quincy was far from a convivial mood. Her irritating dream lingered on in her mind. She had dreamt of Stephen. He could not recognize Quincy, no matter how she tried to get his attention. He found her to be a nuisance and he drove away. Then alone in their driveway, she awoke.

Quincy swiped a slice of bacon from the pile, went to the kitchen and poured a cup of coffee, and left. As she showered, she thought about running the Life Boat. Last evening, in his office, she knew what Price was going to say. She knew it. He was going to Thailand to find Olivia. He wanted her to be the acting director while he was away. Another life completely, she thought, just what her Ex claimed, without a clue why. Thus, the outrageous challenge. As Quincy put on her makeup, she realized at breakfast this morning Jane was wearing men's clothes and Mary Osborne was wearing a dress. My God she thought, the earth quakes and they react as if innocence can be put back on, like a pair of well-worn jeans or a favorite summer dress. She smiled at herself in the mirror. But as with times when Quincy was convinced her insight was on the mark, this was a wide miss.

Quincy returned to the dining area, and still all were sitting around the table. The most severe of the residents either held a stare of unknowing or searched around for something knowable. They grunted, some drooled. But they smiled when Grace and Petrol performed for them. Some laughed loud and pounded the table when Petrol presented to Grace a tin can that once opened, green and yellow toy snakes sprung into the air with goofy faces. Petrol would only bring his BS button when Father Price was not present. They loved the BS button. And some could say 'Bull Shit' with the fervor of a screaming sports fan. This morning Grace and Petrol were acting especially silly, as if something extraordinary was occurring, or had occurred.

Jane and Mary Osborne sat by themselves at a nearby table. Quincy sat with them, watching Grace and Petrol carry on for the residents.

"Where's Father Price?" asked Quincy.

Mary Osborne was enjoying Grace and Petrol's performance.

"You can call me James. I was born James, not Jane." James smiled.

"Where's Cart?" asked Quincy.

"The chapel," said James.

"It's where the piano is—but he wants it moved here in this room. He doesn't like playing in the chapel, and he can't be in The Syndromes because, well you know why, so he can't play the piano in their practice room."

"So, Cart plays piano…" said Quincy.

"Like a fiend!" James beamed. "His left hand, is like, like, hypersonic, man. Hypersonic."

Then she stood up. Her walk from the dining area to the chapel was as if in a trance in the desert. The high clouds were a continuing relief.

From just outside the main doors, she could hear Cart playing. She opened the door and out poured the tightest, fastest boogie woogie groove any piano player ever played in the chapel, the Life Boat, and who knows how far away. Cart was bent over, as the great Bill Evans bent over his sophisticated chords. But whereas Bill was many times in a meditative heroin state, Cart played sober, as if it was the last day on Earth. Sweat poured from him. The groove was contagious; a deaf man would have little choice but to shake it. Whether or not Cart noticed Quincy's entrance, Quincy was uncertain. She sat close, to watch him closely. When Cart tired, he still kept the left hand playing the rhythm, albeit slow, resting and thinking what and how to play the next bit.

Then Cart resumed.

Unheard, Mr. Galvin Salvus now sat down behind Quincy. Cart played on.

"Bravo, Bravo!" exclaimed Mr. Salvus, the chapel echoing his vigorous clapping. Quincy let out a cry in shock, becoming livid. Cart stopped playing, closed the lid, grabbed his new walking stick, the pole used to carry the Crucifix in processions, but without the Crucifix atop, and left in silence by the side aisle. Upon passing by, Cart motioned as if tipping an invisible hat. Sweat streamed down his face, and his breathing was labored.

"May I join you?" Salvus said. Quincy's silence ignored, he got up to sit next to her.

He wore a black suit and white shirt, without a tie. Tailored--expensive, but not ostentatious. Tall men in black suits attracted Quincy. Her Ex, for example.

"Father Price canceled my interview?" asked Salvus.

Quincy was disoriented. She was upended, with no anchor to give her any perspective of what was happening. Sitting in a chapel pew, now quiet, whereas a few moments ago Cart was pounding out boogie woogie piano as if surrendering an offering. Was he playing to God, playing for God? His left hand rhythm locking her in a swaying trance, and Quincy felt powerless to escape.

Quincy and Salvus sat in silence. Quincy's mind could not stop, her thoughts were fragmented and racing past her consciousness in no sensible manner.

Salvus touched her arm. She recoiled, her powerlessness not abating.

He said, "I know why you are here."

"You are here to interview me," he said.

"No, Father Price conducts interviews." Quincy remained looking at the altar.

"He is not here and you are here."

"You have to come back when Father Price is available." Quincy felt outside her body--yet present and aware of her surroundings. She became dizzy.

"He is superb. I love boogie woogie piano," said Salvus, now turning to face Quincy, who was not going to turn and face him.

"You said I'm here because I'm to interview you," said Quincy.

"Yes."

"Why are you here?" asked Quincy, now turning to face him. Her reaction to his presence came through in her inflection. It seemed to be the only question ever asked at the Life Boat.

"I have transferred more than sufficient funds to cover my necessities."

"How do you know where to transfer the funds?" she said.

"The Life Boat accepts donations."

"I don't have any authority to approve such things. I am not that person," said Quincy.

"No background check? I know a background check is required," she said.

"What do you want to know?"

"Why are you here?"

"Who are you?" Quincy regained only her attitude.

"I am The Fallen Angel."

"What does that mean?" Quincy's vulnerability was exposed in an instant. Fear overcame her narcissism.

"Devil."

Quivering, Quincy said, "Brilliant interview answer desiring to be an assistant in a Catholic house whose mission is to administer to the severely mentally disabled. You win a chocolate chip cookie."

"I love chocolate chip cookies," said Salvus.

"I am no longer what I was," he continued.

"Yes, I see. Fully certified fucking dangerous crazy. I demand to see that certification," said Quincy.

"I have been forgiven. I am anew."

Quincy became terrified when she realized just then her disbelief was unconvincing to herself. Looking straight ahead, like a horse with blinders, she said, "And your penance is to bring your bullshit here? In this place? Upon me? You know Petrol has the Bull Shit Red Button and won't hesitate to press it. He's uncanny at detecting bull shit."

"Mercy. It's a gift beyond any comparison."

"So you say." Quincy was losing her peripheral vision.

"And Hell?" asked Quincy.

"Hell is hell."

"But you're not in Hell, or are you saying this is Hell?" She tensed every muscle not to faint.

"This is not Hell."

"And the reason I'm here is because I am to interview you?"

"Yes."

"Why me?"

"You know that answer, Quincy."

"I'm special?"

"You are singular."

"And the difference is...?"

"Millions of miles different."

"How so?"

"We share a similar weakness."

"What?"

"Being Quincy is not special. But being Quincy is singular--in that you are at the highest level."

"I ask your permission to let me stay."

"My permission?" asked Quincy.

"Yours alone."

Quincy then stood, holding firm to the pew in front of her. Leaving the chapel without collapsing in fear—that was her immediate concern. She thought of strangling either White or Gray. That is, only after they served the best wine in the world. A good time to be a whiskey drinker.

"Thank you," said Salvus. He followed behind her to the dining area.

"We need our priest back," said Quincy, aware Salvus was close behind.

"And no, you're not qualified to fill in."

"Why does the Life Boat require a priest?" asked Salvus.

Quincy stopped and turned around, facing Salvus. His calmness served only to unmoor Quincy from any semblance of control. Maybe strangling him would make her feel better, she thought. He was skinny enough to take on.

"Because this place needs a religious director. And you're not qualified," she said, very much wanting to punch his wan smile down his throat.

"Have the families of the residents stopped by to check on them since the earthquake?"

"No. They all made calls to see if everyone was safe," she said.

"Don't you find that disconcerting?" asked Salvus.

"I don't know how to find that," said Quincy, now turning back around and walking to the dining area.

"You will not tell anyone the preposterous story you told me about yourself. Pick another lie to tell the others. You cannot visit any of the residents in their rooms."

She said, "You know about gardening. Create a garden. There's plenty of space in the back of this property, and water is no problem. Grow things we all like to eat. Start today. No snakes."

"As you wish."

In her room, Quincy vomited until she gagged on her bile. She freshened up and returned to the chapel to wait for Father Price. Quincy felt safest in the pews.

Father Price finally arrived. They sat in silence, until Quincy spoke.

"Will you get another priest to come by and say Mass and do priestly things? And we *do* have to have a doctor around here. Who will that be?"

"You're not going to quit on me, I take it?" said Father Price. No point in telling him about Salvus' admission. How would the conversation start?

"I'm in the chapel, otherwise I'd tell you to fuck off," she said, relying on anger to get her mind straight. Still nauseous, her throat raw from the bile. He laughed.

"Priests are in very short supply."

"And doctors?" asked Quincy.

"Less so," he said.

"Victor can help."

"He's difficult."

"To you, maybe. I have found him very approachable."

"You're difficult," said Quincy.

"But clearly, your Olivia doesn't think so," she added.

"And what are you, Quincy?"

"I know exactly what I am."

"And I am also working hard to be nice, Father."

"It shows."

"Quincy, you have resources you can call on. You're going to need to call on them. I'm praying for you to do just that. Your self-confidence is your wealth, as you rarely fail to demonstrate. Who knows, maybe Mr. Salvus will pitch in to help run this place."

"You left me here to interview him? That's *your* job!" yelled Quincy.

Father Price said, "I had no doubt you could do it. You'll be the one to decide now."

"I know nothing about him. I met him on a pier fishing. He's ancient. He's frail and thin. His hands shake. I doubt he is who he says he is." Telling Father Price what Salvus told Quincy was out of the question. He'd never believe her, and only rile her up more with further talk about Salvus, which she would not permit.

"Your decision," said Father Price.

"Why are you praying for me?"

"I pray for everyone here," said Price.

"Do I need prayers said for me?"

"Doesn't everyone?" he said.

"Tell me Father, why is it that you don't discourage all those delusional souls out there who pray for divine intervention to cure a loved one, or maybe themselves, from dying of cancer? People pray every second of the day for a miracle. Why would you not discourage that type of insanity?"

"I don't encourage praying for miracle cures."

"But you don't discourage, do you?"

"Who am I to discourage anyone from praying?"

"What do you pray when you pray for me?"

"I pray that Grace is extended on to you to strengthen you in times of difficulty and stressful uncertainty in order for you to act to best serve those you are serving. "

"I certainly don't pray that you be cured of your abundant narcissism—now you might call that delusional."

Father Price stood. "I have some tasks I need to complete. This evening after supper I wish to sit down with you and go over some details about how the Life Boat operates, bills we pay, and the family members we keep in contact with. They all have their particular needs regarding how they are kept informed of their loved ones living here."

He left. She sat and stared at the crucifix above the altar. The crucifix, altar, candles, stations of the cross along the walls, the pews and kneelers; inside the chapel was an alien experience, with no points of reference to any connection to what mattered to her. But what mattered to Quincy was becoming alien to her now. Her only reference was memories of her Ex. She missed him very much. Stephen was all she considered to be meaningful.

Chapter 13

Saturday morning.

Band practice.

Father Price departed.

Salvus moved in.

The Syndromes now had a guitar player and piano player. Gone was the banging on drums with no ability to create rhythm and a plodding two note bass line at pounding volume. On arrival were James and Cart's guitar and piano interplay, with Mary Osborne accepting limited instruction from James on which four notes she must play. The other members no longer participated in percussion, seemingly content to watch, stare about, and perhaps listen.

The reason for men in the lineup was due to James accepting Mary Osborne's proposal to marry. James was worried the name Jane may have stuck, no matter how many times James asked Mary to call him by his given name. Mary always liked the name Jane and told him so. It was only when he threatened to also wear a wedding dress that Mary relented, adding another promise to the wedding vows. Rock bands always had lineup changes, for reasons explained and otherwise. But they still needed a drummer.

Grace and Petrol explained all this to Quincy, who stood outside the rehearsal room listening--gob smacked by the suddenness of what was happening. They told her she no longer needed to audition. A creeping onset of hysteria amplified her disorientation--no sleep the night before and meandering too long on an empty stomach. They escorted her to the dining area and Petrol hustled on ahead to get White and Gray into action.

"We met Salvus this morning," said Grace, offering his arm to her unsteady walk. She refused.

"He's already living with us?" asked Grace.

"Is that wise? He is very strange. Scary. Who is he?"

"Father Price decided," she lied.

"I'm very worried," said Grace.

"How are the residents?" asked Quincy.

"Petrol and I will be making our rounds soon. They all were fine at breakfast."

"I'm very worried. Thailand is in heavy turmoil."

Stopping short of the dining area entrance, Quincy said, "Grace, don't get yourself into a state." He paused, and then laughed.

"A state?" smiled Grace.

"You know, so you don't have a seizure," she said, missing her own play on words.

"My particular worry doesn't cause a seizure, just diarrhea."

"I can't prevent you worrying, so I'm not going to try. Now I am going to try to eat breakfast. No more diarrhea talk."

White and Gray delivered breakfast and coffee. They waited nearby, just out of her view. Quincy was convinced she intimidated the robots, finding small pleasure. She ate, thinking about her next encounter with Salvus. She also thought about communicating with her Ex, for his help.

Chapter 14

"Moved in?" Salvus was standing in the office doorway, the brilliant daylight causing Quincy to squint toward his tall silhouette.

"Making sure bills are being paid around here." Quincy's eyes returned to the desktop computer screen. She found nothing personal. A contact list for all the residents and their families, and only official correspondence in the few emails Price kept in the 'in' and 'sent' folders. Quincy found the account that paid the bills. Everything was set up for automatic payment. All seemed in order.

As her eyes adjusted, she saw that Salvus was in clean clothes. He came in and sat down on the cushioned chair.

"Finish gardening already?"

"For today, yes. I tire easily these days. A week or so and it will be ready for planting. Wonderful soil here."

"The necessary tools have been delivered, along with a small storage building. The fabricated buildings are exceptional."

"Who pays for all this?" asked Quincy, avoiding looking at Salvus.

"Everything has arrived. The motor tiller is thrilling to operate."

"Let's go see the progress then," said Quincy.

Quincy hated nervousness. She was too afraid to think about thinking about him. Outside was quiet and hot. Quincy was growing accustomed to both, although unimaginable months ago. It was a garden in the making. Sections for different vegetables and herbs. The fabricated storage building came with a small office and was air-conditioned.

"I'm here because you are here," said Salvus. Quincy ignored him.

"Power will be available in three days," said Salvus, standing next to those already gathered.

"We watched them do this!" said Petrol.

Quincy looked at Grace, who said, "A dozen men arrived at dawn, opened the fence, and began to work. They just left." The fence had no appearance of being opened; where there was no gate, there was now a gate in the fence.

Grace, Petrol, James and Tall Mary, along with Cart, were standing in the new garden.

Quincy looked at Salvus. He smiled. Close to him, she had never seen someone so old. She shivered. She endured him explaining anything to her.

"You refer to him as your Ex."

"You know him?" asked Quincy.

"You refer to Stephen, your husband? You don't say his name? Has he done great harm to you?"

"Are you one of his special lawyers?"

The others remained oblivious to Quincy and Salvus. Excited, they continued talking amongst themselves.

Salvus laughed.

"Your husband and I never met, and yes, I would be an excellent lawyer."

"I see how this type of standing around causes you to tire easily," said Quincy. Salvus laughed again, this time the others took note. His utterance was unusual.

"Tomorrow there's no priest to say Mass," said Quincy, looking beyond the garden, to the end of the property, and out to the mountains. She wondered if the earthquake wrecked the VacTrain line. Quincy wanted to ask Salvus no questions. He asked too many. Any answers to his questions did nothing to allay her fear of him, and she avoided him as much as she could.

****

There were days at a time when the residents were very difficult to assist--as if they synchronized their gestures of discontent, and their sadness. What was hidden from everyone was well hidden, and rarely discovered. They either could only say a few words or grunt, groan, motion, or spit to communicate. Not knowing what they felt or thought was equally upsetting and the assistants many times became as helpless as the residents.

Grace ensured each resident received the proper medication and Mary Osborne did the rest, but she was not having success administering medications. She was as patient as Dr. Pernell, but patience was not effective in getting medications swallowed when they refused to cooperate.

Days ago, in the chapel, all the residents and their families were gathered at Quincy's insistence. She announced that Father Price was away and she had no contact with him or Dr. Pernell.

The most vocal of the family members interrupted each other, demanding answers as to Father's whereabouts and return, why he was impossible to contact, why they had not been informed sooner, and how it came to be that Quincy had taken charge of the Life Boat. Not all the family members reacted in this manner. Grace stopped paying attention, distracted at the thought he never had a chance to read the Epistles and Gospel during Mass.

None of them however, were willing to move their kin from the Life Boat back to their homes. And none of them noticed Salvus sitting in the far back pew. He focused on Quincy and her failed attempt to mollify their indignation. James knew the reason the residents were in their state. It started the previous Sunday in the chapel when the most vocal members of the families were shouting their displeasure at Quincy. As their voices raised, the family members they placed in the Life Boat further slumped and lowered their heads. Yes, thought James, the residents' collective sadness started on Sunday morning.

****

Two days later, in the early afternoon, Mary Osborne's door knock ended Quincy's ten-minute nap.

"Come with us," said Mary, with no thought of her interruption. Quincy looked at James for any clue as to where they wanted to take her but he gave none. She wasn't sure she wanted to ask. It didn't seem to be an emergency. James never displayed any urgency, as if he had altogether abandoned the reflex. Mary Osborne always seemed in an urgent state. Not a panic, not frantic, but a compulsion to move towards something, or some place, other than where she was. As if a low fear, ever present, would rise unless she moved elsewhere—many occasions just moving to the opposite side of a room.

James could stay in one place all day and feel nothing. But if Mary wanted to move, James followed—as was the case at the moment.

In silence, Quincy got up and went to the bathroom mirror to adjust herself. Other than the evenings right after dinner, she spent almost no time with the residents in their rooms.

Hiding the nameplate on the door, Mary asked, "Do you know her name?" Quincy stared at Mary.

Mary removed her hand and pointed to the first letter in her name.

"Catherine," said Mary, "Spelled with a 'C'."

Catherine, twenty-three, was tiny and spindly. To prevent her from chewing her thin brown hair, it was kept short. With assistance, she could walk, but with great difficulty. Her muscular control was best only in the mornings. Catherine was just able to control her bowels and bladder. Her facial expressions were dramatic, and when she smiled, rare could another smile compare. Her teeth were porcelain white and in straight alignment, producing a shock to anyone upon their first encounter with her. Her tepid wave to Mary

Osborne, James, and Quincy was delivered with no smile.

"Catherine loves to talk. Cart says he knows what she says, but I can't understand her," said Mary, bending over to hug Catherine, producing a reluctant smile.

Mary said, "I think she likes Cart, but not like I like James. She is not ready to get married."

"What has become of the wall paper her mother said was her favorite?" Quincy did remember her mother's insistence that Catherine loved a particular wallpaper pattern. She brought rolls of it when she arrived. Quincy could not think of an uglier wallpaper color and design.

Mary said, "She threw a roll of it across her room and spit." Her bedroom walls remained bare, and the bleak institutional look struck an angry chord with Quincy. She knelt down to look at Catherine.

"Catherine, my name is Quincy and I am very happy you are here!" This was Quincy's performance of enthusiasm and welcoming she had perfected as a teenager. A guaranteed winner in any setting, with any audience. The perfect bait for hungry fish she so much desired to catch. Catch and release was for fools believing they exercised wisdom in their appointed earthly, nature loving benevolence. Quincy caught to consume.

Catherine looked away. Quincy's bait was ignored—not just by Catherine, but also by everyone at the Life Boat. But she didn't believe Catherine ignored her--no--something else caused her to look away. Quincy stood up, smiling at Catherine. She remained focused on Catherine to stave off an onset of panic. Whatever Catherine was thinking, Quincy could not imagine more distant thoughts. She believed the span of distance was unfathomable, a distance of a billion light years or more. And within this span, how much was filled with loneliness? It was only loneliness that Quincy thought of when she saw Catherine. There was no stronger border than the border between the thoughts and desires of anyone, and anyone else. But bridges existed across borders that routed through narrow streets to neighborhoods of the mind, and loneliness was a familiar neighborhood to anyone. Now Quincy was afraid to look at the other residents. Quincy grew angry knowing it was at the Life Boat where she became fearful. First it was Salvus, and now the residents. But she could not go back to her former life, because she had conquered that world. But she knew her victory was nothing of nothing, and any illusion otherwise would fall flat, as if on brittle stilts. She missed her Ex terribly, and with the fear of his remaining forever distant, she began to cry.

Then Catherine turned her head and looked at Quincy. Catherine smiled. Quincy rushed from the room.

Six minutes later she was in her van, pulling out of the driveway, heading west.

Tall Mary stayed with Catherine for hours, talking to her about her plans to marry James, and the kind of dress she dreamed of, and the music she wanted to hear during the wedding. She asked Catherine to be a bridesmaid.

James sat and listened.

Catherine smiled.

Chapter 15

The pier was crowded, as if no earthquake occurred, and Quincy fished until nightfall. She watched the blue sky be overtaken by varying hues of orange amongst the high swirly, wispy clouds. The breeze cooled her. The wine buzzed her mind. Other than being grateful for no thoughts, she caught nothing until sunset--then her pole tip bent below her feet, and she almost lost grip. She knew what was on her line and she was afraid the line would break. Quincy had let her bait lay on the bottom. Out of the water rose a thrashing guitarfish, over five pounds, part ray, part shark. The light test line would not hold--she knew it. She hated the thought of the line breaking and her catch plunging back into the ocean with a hook in its mouth, hopefully not swallowed. But the pier lights were not bright enough for Quincy to tell if the guitarfish swallowed the hook. Then the line broke. She cried out and turned away as the guitarfish smacked the water. She grabbed the empty wine bottle and threw it in the ocean. Those on her side of the pier booed in unison, as if in a mono boo choir.

Otherwise, it was a gorgeous evening on the pier.

Leaving, she flipped her jacket hood around her head, pulling it forward. A few drinkers and fishermen called her some choice names, hyphened epithets, most names including bitch. They knew she was Quincy Lane.

In her van, Quincy cried. She twisted open another bottle of wine and poured a glass. Now thoughts rushed her, splayed across her no longer blank canvas of a mind, in drips, drops, and splashes. Having a conscious was one thing, being reminded of it was quite another. Why now--to be aware of being conscious of anything? What good is it? For what purpose?

She spun out of the parking lot, but before exiting into the traffic, she stopped in a skid. Quincy engaged auto drive for the first time in her life. Confirming in her destination, Quincy reclined her seat. Instead of another glass of wine, she tossed her empty glass over to the passenger seat where it clinked against the wine bottle but did not shatter. In no time she fell asleep. She was on the road--with plenty of other drunks.

The alert sounded. Ding Ding Ding, Ding Ding Ding—in chromatic ascending and descending tones. These chimes woke Quincy five minutes before her destination. Approaching the gate, she gave a voice command to her PED, and the gate opened. The house was dark. She did not permit the lights to go on, and in the kitchen, she poured the remaining wine from her bottle into the sink and left the bottle on the counter. Passing the vast, open living room, where one enjoyed a very pleasant view of the ocean through a wide picture window, she entered the master bedroom. First, she opened his dresser drawers inside the walk-in closet. The lights came on. She counted his underclothes, folded and stacked. She then ran her hands across his suits, near fifty in all, and surveyed the shoes underneath. Afterwards she lay atop their bed, on his side. Quincy closed her eyes. She cleared her mind of unwanted thoughts, labeling all of them as nothing, for there was nothing she felt any compunction to do one way or the other to affect a consequence of any thoughts. Normally so easy, so effortless. But now, Quincy began thinking that maybe she *ought* to do something. Nothing in particular, but *something*. She smelled Stephen's evening scent. She fell asleep, thanking him that his scent still lingered.

Chapter 16

Quincy awoke in a panic, from a dream she wanted to play back again and again. She shed her clothes, tossing them on their bed. She showered and made herself presentable in public, as always. Dressed, she sipped coffee in the darkness, looking out over the ocean. There was no moonlight to illuminate the water.

Grace's thirteen phone calls to Quincy had gone unanswered. Late the evening prior Grace found her phone on the nightstand in her Life Boat room. In the early morning hours his panic changed to sadness, believing Quincy had left them, as Father and Olivia had.

Salvus sat on his bed. He couldn't sleep. He was uncertain if Quincy was returning. He got up and packed his belongings. Without Quincy, Salvus would not remain at the Life Boat. He was to remain with her.

Quincy returned to the Life Boat at four am. Both Grace and Salvus heard her van pull up in the driveway. Both opened their doors, peeking to see Quincy below, walking around the courtyard. They saw the light come on in the dining area and heard her bark out to Gray to make her coffee. Grace gave thanks to God and went back to bed. Salvus unpacked his belongings and put them away. He sat back on his bed, wondering if he should give thanks. It seemed such a trivial matter to him, but Salvus knew better with Him. Salvus thought about his hesitation to give thanks. He needed to work on that. No doubt. He got undressed and lay down. Keeping her at the Life Boat may be the right course—in order to remain with her, he thought, because--maybe this is the place. Talking with her is difficult without her casting me out. She is not going to understand why I am here. She will not believe me.

He fell asleep.

Quincy got little sleep. Sitting on a chair near the chapel entrance, she watched the sunrise, knowing it was going to be a hot one. In front of her was the new garden. She had no opinion of it, one way or the other. Quincy returned to her room and worked herself into a sweat by exercising in intense, short intervals, all the types of movements she paid her expensive trainer to teach her. And then all the yoga poses her yoga teacher taught her. After showering and preparing for the day, a few beads of sweat dripped down the sides of her face as she joined Mary Osborne and James to get the residents ready for breakfast. Mornings were not easy as most of the residents were barely able to take care of themselves. Bed linens

114

were changed daily. After breakfast, Petrol and Cart did the laundry. Grace was not present for breakfast, and therefore no one led the morning prayers. Salvus arrived after all were seated.

"Damn robots," said Quincy to herself, with a mouth full of scrambled egg whites.

Nodding towards White and Gray, now serving breakfast to the residents, Quincy said, "And we have little choice—we need those two damn things to do more with the residents. I don't care what the Regulators say. Plus, I want to rename them. I want to call them Thing 1 and Thing 2--maybe slap a number on the back and front."

No one responded to Quincy. Mary and James were having their own private conversation. Catherine enjoyed Cart helping her eat breakfast. The rest were being fed by Petrol, as he rotated between the residents as if in slow motion, which was the ideal tempo for all the women.

"That's settled, then," said Quincy. No one was listening.

Turning to Salvus she said, "Unless you know the kind of someone or ones that are willing to live here, I would like you to find us some more robots, the kind that can help with the helpless. God knows we need some help. You have connections--I know you do. The garden, for example."

Salvus bit into his toast with strawberry jam, his favorite. He nodded to Quincy.

"Thanks," she said. His silence made her no less fearful of him but gave her room to breathe. Salvus knew this. She then let her mind be filled with what she believed needed to be done to run the Life Boat. The prime importance was finding a new priest, a task she could never give to Salvus. Only one person she knew in her life attended Mass--much less knew a priest. God was for those who were not like her. But Stephen would know someone who knew.

"We need a priest," announced Quincy.

"I know a priest," said Cart. He finished helping Catherine with breakfast and started eating his own. It was now cold eggs, sausage and potatoes. Heating up was a task White or Gray would not hesitate to execute, but Cart didn't mind. Having any sort of breakfast was still a significant luxury. He was determined not to take anything for granted. A life pledge.

"I know that Marjorie Bentham, who is a colossal pain in the ass, knows the priest. He's from Syria. Escaped the civil war, miracle by miracle, according to her. He's very old. But he's a priest. I met him twice. A Melkite. But you'll have to deal with Marjorie Bentham."

"A Melkite?" asked Salvus.

"A Melkite," said Cart.

"What's a Melkite?" asked Quincy.

Cart shrugged. Hesitant, Quincy glanced at Salvus.

Salvus concentrated on spreading butter and jam on his remaining piece of toast. Taking his first bite, Salvus noticed Cart nodding at him, attempting to get him to say something. Quincy stared at Cart.

"Melkites descend from the See of Antioch—the first See being St. Peter the Apostle."

"See?" asked Cart.

"A recognized authority," said Salvus. He desired another piece of toast.

"Where can I find him?" said Quincy.

"I don't know," said Cart. He finished his breakfast and pulled away from the table to take his plate to the kitchen. Catherine turned to watch him.

"I have to go ask this Marjorie Bentham woman, then?"

Cart nodded and walked to the kitchen.

Calling to Cart, Quincy asked, "Where do I find her?"

Cart said, "Take me fishing and I'll show you where."

"Show me where, then I'll take you fishing."

"Deal. Catherine wants to go too." When she heard her name, Catherine smiled.

Salvus excused himself and left the dining area.

Petrol, Mary, and James situated the residents in the living area, in the same large room as the eating table, but on the opposite side. Tobacco colored leather sofas and cushioned chairs were arranged around a large, blue turquoise area rug of Oriental design. Although speakers were inset in the ceiling above, no music was playing. Quincy never asked Father Price why no video screen was permitted. She was going to place an order for one today, she decided, also, deciding a piano was required, since Cart played.

Now, a large truck rumble rattled the windows. Quincy went to the far window. A cement mixer and crew were outside, coming onto the premises through the same gate as the workers who were building the garden. She saw Salvus looking up, talking with the truck driver. The driver motioned with his arm, both nodded to each other, and then Salvus backed away and let the driver proceed. Soon, Petrol, Mary, and James turned the furniture towards the large window so all the residents could watch the goings on. The wide swath through the middle of the garden was prepped for laying down a concrete pathway, all the way to the end of the property line.

Leaving them, Quincy went to the office. She wasn't minding the surprises Salvus brought to the

Life Boat. She thought about Grace. Then, he came down the stairs.

"Monique is not well," Grace said. He looked as tired as his voice. Quincy didn't know Monique was not at breakfast, or that Grace had not slept that night. Recalling now, Quincy guessed she was in her thirties, very thin with an almond shaped face, and brown hair. She could speak some and could almost take care of herself. Monique didn't care for Grace and Petrol, much preferring Mary's attention and assistance. But these days Mary was preoccupied with James. Grace knew this.

"How so?" asked Quincy.

"She is moaning, looks very pale, more pale than usual, and won't leave her bed. She refuses to eat or drink anything."

"What do you suggest?" said Quincy.

"We got on well here with Dr. Pernell being a psychiatrist. She could do regular doctor things too," said Grace.

"I'm going to get Tall Mary. She'll know better."

Quincy waited until Grace returned with Mary. She knew the women needed a doctor on call here. An emergency room was not the place for them, or a regular hospital, she thought. Maybe a Catholic hospital, but Quincy thought they had closed and moved elsewhere. They were nudged away from this area.

Embarrassed, Mary had forgotten about Monique this morning. She galloped up the stairs to Monique's room, telling Quincy not to come with her.

Quincy said to Grace, "You look like hell. Eat something and get some sleep."

"We need a doctor here," he said, and walked away.

Chapter 17

On Sunday, in their chapel, Quincy addressed the families of the residents.

"I have been unable to contact both Father Price and Dr. Pernell. I've tried calling, messaging—nothing. You all have their phone numbers too. You've not heard from either of them?"

Most shook their heads, a few spoke up, saying no.

"If you know of one who is willing to say Mass on Sunday, let me know."

"You all have doctors. You will have to make arrangements to get your loved ones to your doctors."

Quincy anticipated the murmuring and their irritation. They were predictable. She counted off to herself how long before someone objected to her being in charge. She guessed thirty seconds. And almost to the second, Quincy was right. So too was she right in who she guessed would speak first. It was that squashed bowling pin of a woman—Short Mary's mother.

"Mrs. Lane? The famous Quincy Lane in the news—not so much these days--but you were always in our faces! The same person who is so successful in getting all that worldwide attention?"

"Mrs. Lane, I ask you, why are you in charge here?"

The chapel became silent, a few of the family members heads nodded. Salvus, in the far pew, believed he was being tested. Cart, across the aisle from Salvus, sat bent over, barely containing his laughter. He could not wait for what came next. Petrol sensed Grace's anxiousness. Mary and James were preoccupied with themselves. She placed James's hand on her belly.

Quincy announced, "Oh, and one more thing, please find someone to be the new director of the Life Boat. I'm leaving today." Quincy glanced at Grace, who was turning pale. As the family members began to snort and become incensed, Quincy caught Grace's eye and gave him an assured wink. No one else saw her. She prayed Grace would not have a seizure. Then she realized what she had done. It was her first time she ever remembered saying an earnest prayer, a prayer for someone else. She dismissed all those times she prayed for foolish things, like her rivals faces filling with bulbous pimples when she was not getting the proper attention she demanded...and other wishes of malevolent nature.

Five times Short Mary's mother stood and sat down, being pulled on by another one of the family members, whispering in her ear some urgent thoughts. Quincy watched them all; their faces displaying shock, disdain, anger, and affronts to their righteousness.

Once more, Quincy winked at Grace. Sill pale, he offered a weak hand wave.

"Grace, please come up here and lead us in a prayer service." Addressing the families, she said, "Let us pray."

Grace came up front and Quincy placed her hand on his shoulder and squeezed. She stepped down and walked to the rear of the chapel along the side aisle, glancing at Salvus, and stood by the doors. Salvus turned his head to watch Quincy. As Grace began to read an epistle from St. Paul, she left the chapel.

Chapter 18

Quincy audibled directions Cart had given her to the van's navigational system. She wanted him to go with her but resisted the temptation at the last moment to beckon Cart as she left the chapel. As Quincy passed by Salvus, she noticed his worry. The possibility of Salvus being other than what Quincy believed him to be, by his own declaration, brought only a very slight relief to her fear of him. She'd take any relief she could get.

Motoring on, Quincy adjusted her hair in the mirror, realizing she was long overdue to visit her stylist. Unacceptable, she knew, pounding the dashboard with both fists. But a calm then came over her. Her pounding fists seemed to expel her extreme dissatisfaction of her physical appearance. Then, the realization of this calm angered Quincy. Anger was a fuel for Quincy's purpose. But she was in no mood to think about why. All she wanted now was to confront this Marjorie Bentham woman. Quincy was also in no mood to notice her purpose had altered.

Marjorie Bentham was not difficult to find. From a distance, she looked to be directing traffic; waving her arms, delivering commands, and pointing and staring down some of the throng of the city's left behinds who had converged on boxes of giveaway clothes just deposited in the vacant lot next to the Compassionate House for Women. That most of the people obeyed Marjorie Bentham's commands is what Quincy noticed first. She wore worn worker boots, blue jeans over wide hips, an oversized man's chambray shirt with the sleeves rolled up, a double chin, and thick curly grey hair of all shades pulled back in a ponytail just below her stocky shoulders.

Quincy wasn't sure when her beauty left her, but as she approached Marjorie Bentham she decided at some time she may have been attractive.

Scrawled on the boxes was 'Men, Women, Kids.' She ordered three men, two skinny and one fat, whose ages were difficult to guess due to their neglected beards and hard life creases on their faces, to take the boxes into the women's shelter next door.

To the crowd Marjorie Bentham said, "Listen people, the rules have not changed. Come back tomorrow and will've sorted the clothes by sizes and you can get what you need." Her high voice and tone did not match her looks. The crowd soon dispersed, but to nowhere in particular.

"I know who you are," said Marjorie Bentham. Quincy was ready for what she believed to be said next--'you're the ridiculously wealthy woman known the world over for being a beautiful, ridiculously wealthy woman.'

"What do you want?" asked Marjorie Bentham. Quincy was surprised she was wrong, but in an instant, she wasn't.

"The Life Boat needs a priest—and a doctor," said Quincy. Neither had any problem staring at each other, without blinking.

It was Marjorie Bentham's laugh that could make you cover your ears. An explosive grating sound. A release of seething anger, like a volcanic burst of spew.

"You all have that, that priest—and his girlfriend, Olivia Pernell. She's supposedly a psychiatrist, that's a doctor, by the way." Something in her voice, thought Quincy.

"Father Price and Dr. Pernell have been called away and we don't know when they'll return."

"How many residents do you have, maybe six, maybe seven?" asked Marjorie Bentham, now squared up and arms crossed.

"You know how many I deal with down here? Tens of thousands are here. Druggies, crazies, and some of the worst personal decision-makers the world has ever seen are down here. Plus, the coward criminals who hide and prey amongst them all. I don't have your types, thanks to the Government. They're either dealt with or are behind closed doors of their families who won't give them up. You get to have that Life Boat because of a loophole in the law. And you have all the money in the world! I don't have any loophole to work in and don't have rich people giving me money. And they work ten blocks down that way. You can't find a doctor? And you want to steal one of mine?"

"And anyway, what are *you* doing at a place like the Life Boat? Why are you there? Are you that priest's new lover now that Pernell left? Is that it?"

Quincy asked herself how long had this woman been waiting to say all that? To me—or just to anyone? Marjorie spoke in a normal conversational volume, maybe just a little lower than normal. But Quincy knew what was underneath. She would not be fooled.

"Down here it's nothing but infections, oozing pus and blood, and more infections. It's so dirty here, dirt and grime are an extra layer of skin."

"You're clearly looking in the wrong place to steal a doctor. You know where to find them, they live where you live!"

"I'm first looking for a priest. He's a Melkite," said Quincy.

Marjorie Bentham looked left and right, surveying the street, but her arms remained folded across her chest.

"Do you think God's around here? I've been here ten years and I haven't seen one sign of God. Even in these little so-called places of worship around here. I can't see God there, either."

"He is Syrian, a civil war refugee", said Quincy.

"Why am I helping you?"

"He's old."

"Do you know I was supposed to be the director of the Life Boat? I applied for that job, I interviewed for that job--I am overqualified for that job. I'm a nurse practitioner for Christ's sake."

"And you, you of all people—you have that job now?"

"Who told you that?" asked Quincy.

"I know all about the Life Boat. What a pathetic name."

"And Cart is with you now, watch that scheming rat bastard."

"He sent you down here, did he not?" Marjorie Bentham then laughed that laugh. It was too late for Quincy to cover her ears.

Quincy drove to her house. She checked out the contents of the refrigerator, and then poured a glass of red wine. She showered, and finished her wine, lying angled on Stephen's side of the bed, and fell asleep.

Chapter 19

Quincy returned to the Life Boat before dawn the next morning. Cart stopped her walking to the dining area for breakfast. He was excited.

"You talked to her? You told her you're looking for the Melkite?"

"She told me God's not present down there."

"He may not be, I don't know. But I do know word will get out you talked to Marjorie Bentham about the priest. Who knows, he may be looking to add to his tiny flock of Syrians. Most of them moved on. He stayed with those who wouldn't--or couldn't."

Quincy ignored Cart's question about what she thought of Marjorie Bentham. With women, Quincy's instincts were first--rate on physical beauty, and then, how you present your looks to the world. There long had been a serious move to condemn Quincy's thinking--an outdated habit that needed to be not just eliminated but purged on threat of banishment. But she knew better. Some traits of human nature will never change, and in her mind, they shouldn't. Quincy knew it was ridiculous—a longish fad that would die out, hopefully soon. These days you could look fantastic into your late sixties. Quincy estimated she had ten years left to look fabulous. She'd deal with the eleventh year when it came.

"How old is this priest?" asked Quincy.

Cart stayed bent, not bothering to look up.

"He looks as old as Salvus."

"*Who* couldn't move on?"

"What do you mean?" said Cart.

"What Syrians couldn't move on?"

"Hell, I don't know. Some were helpless. Don't ask me."

Cart looked up at Quincy. "I know what you're thinking…"

"You couldn't possibly know what I'm thinking," said Quincy.

"I'm thinking of straightening you out," said Quincy.

Cart stayed bent. He paused. "You straighten me, you break me."

"And…I don't want to be broken."

"Don't get weepy on me, you bent man. I'm relying on you to help me while Father Price and Pernell are away."

"Oh, so you say you like me? You're doing your charisma thing on me? That thing that got you all that attention for so long? That's still your thing?"

"Tell me you believe you can charisma me…I know you think you can," said Cart.

Quincy stared down at him. Cart looked up,

granting permission to Quincy to look into his eyes. The problem with both of them holding their ground was simple; they liked each other. But it bothered the living shit out of Cart. And he had to employ the big coy--with everything he had. In this drama, Quincy was a consummate pro. But in this rare case, being bent served Cart.

"And tell me you're gonna take us fishing."

"Us?" said Quincy.

"Catherine wants to go too, remember," said Cart, and he walked fast and away with a grin disguised as a smirk.

The machine noises made Quincy walk past the dining area and around to the back, where progress on whatever Salvus had in mind—a garden, or something—had the appearance of completion, as if on an impatient schedule. Quincy didn't want to ask further because she wasn't interested. She was preoccupied about getting a priest to agree to stay at the Life Boat, with total unawareness of the rarity of priests in the area. She never thought about religious life, or religious people, or the clergy who served them.

Then she noticed the entire back fence of the property was removed, and some kind of work was being done beyond the property line.

She found Salvus standing alone, watching the

men. Quincy remained at some distance behind Salvus, observing him observe. In the foreground the garden appeared complete; furrowed rows of rich dirt, waiting for planting, maybe for all she knew, some things had already been planted, now just waiting for shoots to show themselves above the earth. The heavy machinery was past the long garden; in the empty space beyond the old Life Boat property line.

Salvus turned around, startling Quincy. He motioned with his hand to join him.

"We are getting that priest here," she said, standing next to him but looking out at the men working.

"You talk to this man?" asked Salvus.

"What do you think about having a Melkite here?" said Quincy.

"It's your decision. Just as it's your decision that I remain, or that I go," he said.

"No, that was Father Price's decision," said Quincy.

"It's your decision," he said.

Not looking at Salvus, but staring straight ahead, Quincy said, "You know full well what my reaction was going to be when you told me who you claim to be."

"What do you expect me to do?" she said.

"A very difficult task—and you cannot do it by yourself. No one can," he said.

Quincy blurted, "You are a terrible life distraction." She began to tremble in her confusion.

"A new euphemism for believing me to be of unsound mind?"

"Sure, call it that."

Quincy said, "Please tell me why the back fencing is down and what these men are doing."

In the long minute waiting for him to reply, they watched men gathered around two concrete mixer trucks pouring a large concrete foundation, while others offloaded building materials.

Finally, Salvus answered. "The land has been purchased all the way to the rising foothills, just before the VacTrain property line." Quincy knew who the buyer was, but asked herself--why? When was this arrangement made? What was Stephen thinking?

"A new extension of the Life Boat...that is what is being built," said Salvus.

"How far is it to the VacTrain?"

"At least two miles," said Salvus."

"So, you believe we're expecting company?" said Quincy.

"And you believe I can't do whatever the hell I supposedly need to do by myself?"

"I do," replied Salvus.

Chapter 20

Without notice, the Melkite showed up. Along with La Nina. But she was predicted, and she came weak, bringing rain and furious snow that covered the mountains. Now there were shoots of different shapes in the garden, although Quincy couldn't be bothered to remember what was planted. Maybe because it was Salvus who told her in their very brief morning garden meetings. How long it would stay green around the region was uncertain. But the change from the drought was calming.

Quincy never kept the office door open. The firm knock was unfamiliar, and when she opened the door she knew who he was--before he declared in a low voice, "I come on conditions."

He was tiny and thin, with a full head of white hair, cropped short, like a military man. His equally white beard was well kept. His black suit fit him well, except his pants stopped at his ankles, as if the tailor had run out of material. Pants too short on a tiny man irritated Quincy. His black shoes looked as if he had walked from Syria, with thick leather soles that had been repaired over and over. An accent was present but Quincy guessed his English was excellent.

Quincy stepped out of the office to see if he was

accompanied by anyone, then she invited him in.

"Quincy Lane," she said, and sat down in the comfortable chair next to the sofa.

"Lonan Ford," he said, holding his hand out, expecting it to be taken.

Quincy motioned him to sit on the sofa. As he sat down she asked, "Ford?"

"Consider me assimilated," said Lonan Ford. His pant legs climbed up when he sat, exposing worn white socks and hairy calves.

"How do I know you're a priest?" Quincy would use Stephen's resources to confirm.

"I am a priest."

"Write your real name here please, where you were born, your age, where you went to school— anything else I can use to verify who you are."

"*I too* have conditions," Quincy added, and took a picture of him with her PED as he wrote.

She sent the picture to Victor, Stephen's primary assistant, asking him to verify Lonan Ford's identity. It was the first time she had contacted Victor by messaging.

"Coffee?" asked Quincy, getting up and going to the small break room where a pot had been already brewed.

"Please," said Lonan Ford. He finished writing and looked around the office. Non-descript, clean, no paintings, and a very tidy desk. Nothing personal to be found.

"It's cream," she said nodding towards the ornate porcelain on the serving tray.

Lonan Ford helped himself to a generous pour.

"A Mr. Cart showed me to your office. I remember him. Hard to forget a man bent parallel to the sidewalk." Lonan Ford's English was excellent.

"Who told you I was looking for you?"

He sipped his coffee, paused, and took another sip. He was in no hurry.

"Do you think Marjorie Bentham told me?" he asked.

"Did she?"

He asked, "Why are you here? You are one of the most recognized women in the world. And Saint Theresa from Calcutta you are most definitely not."

"Oh, I'm nothing compared to Mr. Galvin Salvus. You'll meet him, if you are who you are, and I agree to whatever your conditions are." Quincy was immune from the narcissist dig she knew she heard from Ford. She cared less about him personally, and more about whether he'd last more than a year. He had written he was ninety years old on the paper she put in front of him. He looked ninety, but Quincy noticed a quick energy about him. He looked healthy enough. As to Lonan Ford's question, "Why are you here?" She was beginning to become less irritated. Quincy took a picture of the information he had written out and sent it to Victor.

"Help yourself to more coffee," she said. He poured himself another cup, then after, looked at Quincy to see if she wanted more. She accepted.

"What do you know about the Life Boat?" she asked.

"I know Father Price."

"Oh? Then do you know where he is? He left without notice—Thailand maybe."

"I'm sorry, I don't know where he is."

"You know Dr. Olivia Pernell?"

"Yes."

"What do you think of the name—the Life Boat?"

"I think it's appropriate."

"You don't think it's a stupid name, like I do?" Quincy placed her empty coffee cup on the tray.

"No, it's not stupid."

"Alright, what are your conditions?"

"With me I have some people from my church in Syria."

"How many?"

"I'm unsure, because I'm unsure how many will follow me to this place."

"They followed you out of Syria, didn't they?"

"Yes."

"They are scared."

"Of?"

"Of being taken. Where we are living, we have very little, but we know we are not being looked for."

"Of course not, we stopped looking for your kind," said Quincy.

"Yes, yes, I know, that is why they are frightened about leaving where we are."

"Help me here Mr. Ford—or what do I call you, assuming you are in fact a priest."

"Father Lonan is fine. I assimilate," he said, producing his first smile.

"Father Lonan—here's what we're going to do. You're going to talk and tell me everything you think I want to know."

He stood up in front of Quincy. Behind his back he clasped his hands. Father Lonan walked towards the door, and then back again in front of Quincy. He repeated the sequence. All the while Quincy stared at his short pants and shuddered at the thought of Stephen wearing high waters. But when he spoke, Stephen left her thoughts, and Quincy looked straight at him.

"The United States, a very interesting idea, uniting all of the States. For some time, you are united, for some time you are not. Magnificent Constitution. I have paid close attention to the United States my whole life. In secret. Because--the United States is a great Evil."

He laughed. Quincy appreciated his laugh. This man knew about dramatic pause. Every good priest should. Father Lonan had a natural tremolo in his voice. Quincy liked that.

"I am not Muslim, although my family, and all those families my family was joined with--we lived with Muslims for generations. But I paid close attention to the world. I think it pays to pay attention. I think this is an American phrase."

"I came to realize it would be a matter of time, and likely in my own lifetime, when it would become very dangerous for Christians to remain where we lived. I began to convince my family and my people to leave. Very difficult. No one was happy with the decision. I arranged for passage through Turkey and Europe, with my goal to reach the United States. Very difficult. Many came with me to the United States. And some have severe mental limitations. My sister and I care for them. She is a widow, but much younger."

"How old is she?" asked Quincy.

"My youngest sister, she is eighty-five." Lonan Ford laughed.

Quincy did not.

"She is strong, tiny, but strong," said Ford.

"I desire a parish again. My last parish. And I need

to take care of my people."

"Where do you to live now?" asked Quincy.

"In an apartment close to where Marjorie Bentham works."

"How many are you?"

"There are ten of us in the apartment. Two bedrooms. But only five of us will come here to the Life Boat. My sister, two women, one man, and myself."

"Give me a week," said Quincy, adding, "Can you say Mass this Sunday? Nine am."

"Yes, but I have to be back to celebrate Mass at twelve o'clock." Quincy asked for and copied down Father Ford's phone number.

"Change that, I'll let you know after Mass on Sunday," said Quincy.

"And you *are* going to keep this secret--only you. I can't handle more residents."

"Until perhaps, the new buildings are complete?" said Lonan Ford.

"We'll see about all that," said Quincy, standing to escort him out. He rose quickly, extending his hand. This time she accepted the handshake.

"You like to fish?" asked Ford. A smile appeared on her face as if placed without her consent.

As she escorted the tiny Syrian to the door, James and Tall Mary caught up with them, staying some distance behind, until Father Ford got in the passenger seat of an old Toyota sedan. A tiny old woman was driving.

"Quincy?" said James, holding hands with Mary.

"What?" Quincy responded, still watching Father Ford depart.

"Quincy?" repeated James, "We are going to get married."

Quincy turned around and smiled. For the second time, she couldn't help herself.

The question in her mind was not about Tall Mary and James getting married, but whether to ask Victor to find Father Price and Dr. Pernell. She knew he could find them. Stephen's resources were vast. But confirming their whereabouts circled back to the question that was weighing on her. Why had she stayed at the Life Boat for as long as she had?

Quincy hid these thoughts and presented herself as she hoped Mary and James wanted to see. All three were now smiling at each other.

"Talk to Father Ford after Mass on Sunday. Better get married soon, he's damn old."

Chapter 21

Two complexes, six apartments in length two stories high, built so that the first garden extended between the two new complexes, open, to view the rising hills and mountains in the east. The new buildings were almost complete. Modular construction, composite materials, earthquake resistant, energy renewing—Quincy learned how buildings were made, and the speed in which they could be made. She watched the workers because she had to. Salvus appeared to be dying. His frailty was now stark, his face changed color to gray. Salvus would never speak about his health and Quincy had no intent to inquire. The less he talked to her the better, though, who he was and why he was at the Life Boat were now nagging questions for Quincy--alone at night.

Quickly, Quincy became bored dealing with the workers completing the buildings. With Father Ford's concurrence, she passed the task to his sister, Elacha, with Salvus only tending to the garden. Elacha was very pleased. Another Syrian named Thoman, a tall, thick man in his mid forties, with a full peppered beard and a flat top, assisted Elacha. He was a professional soldier and a casualty of conflict.

Thoman was theatrical when communicating, which made up for his deafness and damaged brain from being too close to shrapnel from the incoming mortar round. The other two Syrians brought to the Life Boat were also casualties of war. Susanna and Rebecca. They were captured and enslaved for only two weeks before rescue—but long enough for unthinkable abuse. Both were born with mental limitations, and their nightmares were dreadful listening that the Life Boat residents endured. Five Syrians in all—the rest elected not to follow. Quincy was relieved. There were now far too many unknowns for her. During her life with her Ex, well compensated employees handled the unknowns.

Elacha and Thoman spoke English, although Thoman's accent was impenetrable. Elacha was a wind-up spring of energy, without needing to be wound up. Spry, with enthusiasm of a twenty year old, she could see past day-to-day trivialities that tempted to stir vain frustration. Quincy avoided the indictment that Elacha denied the decimation of her people in order to ignore the suffering, and instead, believed that Elacha was endowed with long range sight, just a few degrees above the horizon, able to glance down at will at the inescapable tragedy, yet able to escape—because of a duty to relieve the suffering of others. Was Elacha always this way? Quincy thought--yes.

Quincy knew her Ex would have been delighted to know her.

Quincy was pleased with herself for this new thinking. For the first time, she needed to remind herself of her insights hour by hour. Because lately, she wanted nothing other than to return to their home and lie on Stephen's side of the bed, weep, and fall asleep.

Chapter 22

A new priest was living at the Life Boat and celebrating Sunday Mass, and Quincy made sure every parent knew she was responsible. After Mass, Elacha gave them a tour of the new construction project. Another natural in most everything, thought Quincy. Salvus was feeling better, and was up and about, following the construction progress, but he deferred to Elacha and Thoman. There stood Salvus, tall and gaunt, Elacha, tiny, and Thoman, a bruiser.

Tall Mary's only living parent was her father, taller than Salvus, but twice the girth. During the tour, Quincy asked Conrad Osborne to allow everyone else to move ahead of them as Elacha talked about the construction project. The two now trailed the rest of the group.

"Your daughter is getting married." Conrad's knees began to buckle. She punched his fleshy arm. Quincy had no intention of attempting to keep him upright--my God, she thought, the size of the man.

"Don't you think about fainting," she said. "You're going to walk her down the aisle, and give her all the money she'll need, because she may be expecting."

"You are certain?" asked Conrad.

"I am not certain."

145

"Don't you think about having a heart attack either," Quincy said, punching him again, harder.

As they caught up with the group Conrad's face turned from shock to perspiring worry. He paid a steep price to have her daughter's sterilization record falsified— at Mary's mother's insistence. But then again, he thought, he hadn't heard anything over the past few years about the Regulators focusing on the mentally impaired. Not nearly as they did years ago. His wife would have wept for joy over the wedding news. He asked himself how she would feel knowing Mary may have a baby.

Chapter 23

The same day Victor messaged to Quincy that Father Price and Dr. Pernell were in Thailand was the same day Father Ford collapsed and was hospitalized. In a week, James and Tall Mary were to be married.

Salvus was again convinced he was dying. Father Ford agreed to hear his confession. Now Father Ford was in the hospital, under the care of Marjorie Bentham. She was a licensed Nurse Practitioner and Physician's Assistant and claimed the priest as a previous patient. The hospital was eager to have her tend to him.

Quincy instructed Victor to send Father Price and Dr. Pernell a message about James and Mary, and that they needed a priest to conduct the wedding. She wouldn't count on them to attend. Marjorie Bentham, attending to Father Ford, irked Quincy more than anything at the moment. It was Monday, and the week was already full of irritations.

The construction project was stalled over a dispute with the general contractor. Quincy was unconvinced Elacha could handle the situation. Thoman had to be removed from any interaction with the construction crew. He wanted to go on a one-man ass-kicking spree and it took more than Elacha's energy to restrain him.

Quincy had also gained an intolerable amount of weight. But none of these happenings irked her more than relying on Marjorie Bentham.

Over the phone Marjorie Bentham told Quincy, "Father Ford insists that only his sister and Thoman can visit him. And Cart. No one else."

"That includes me?" asked Quincy.

"He didn't mention you."

Quincy hung up. Seeing Marjorie's phone number in her very short list of contacts was irksome. A short quick series of knocks on the office door announced Grace and Petrol. Quincy had not spent much time with them lately. She had been leaving as soon as dinner was finished; skipping communal prayer and watching the nature programs the residents were very fond of. Exhausted, they both fell into the sofa.

"We must show you something," said Grace.

"Now?" said Quincy, not in the mood to do anything, especially her next duty, to pay a visit to Salvus and check in on him.

It had become an unspoken agreement. The original residents were looked after by Quincy, Grace, Petrol, James, Tall Mary and Cart. The Syrians looked after themselves.

"Please," said Petrol. He seldom addressed Quincy.

"We don't see you do your exercises and all those funny things you do in the morning," said Petrol. Quincy was not pleased. She spent thousands of dollars learning to do those funny things.

"Where we going?" said Quincy.

"The chapel," said Grace.

"Tell me it's a miracle," she said.

Sweat formed on their brows during the short walk to the chapel. Quincy looked at the construction progress. The buildings were complete except for the interior, and that is where the dispute centered around. Too many toilets added to the plan that supposedly was final.

Inside, the chapel was cool and quiet. She wanted to sit in a pew by herself, maybe lie down and sleep. Grace motioned to follow him to the sacristy. Once there, he went to a door that had been hidden by the vestment wardrobe. Quincy didn't care why the door was hidden or how or why Grace knew about the door. Her thoughts were bouncing from Father Ford to Salvus, the construction project dispute, whether Father Price and Olivia would ever return, Stephen, and the massive irritation known as Marjorie Bentham. But in the chapel, she thought about Stephen.

Behind the door was a storeroom. Grace turned on the lights. A large canvas cloth was covering the surprise. Grace and Petrol flipped off the covering and underneath were four more Cynths. Quincy stared at the Cynths, remembering something. Stephen tried to introduce them into their house, and by the end of the first day Quincy had led it out into the street where a garbage truck smacked it into a neighbor's privacy wall, sending parts everywhere. It made her day.

"We need these Cynths. They can do amazing tasks. We need them," said Grace.

"To do what?" said Quincy, hiding her relief. Salvus?

"Help us with our residents. They can do amazing things," said Grace.

"Not going to help me with my Marjorie Bentham problem, not going to be able to officiate over James and Tall Mary's wedding, not going to finish the construction project," said Quincy.

Confused about her first problem, Grace paused, and then exclaimed, "We get them programmed to assist our residents!"

"And the Regulators? What happens when they find out?" said Quincy, now hiding a smile.

"Once those damn things are on line, they'll be here in a flash. They are not licensed and registered and you know the Regulators are all about licensing and registering."

"Yes, but you have Victor," said Grace.

"What about Victor?" she said. Quincy never cared for Victor.

Grace pleaded, "He can find someone who can do the *discrete* programming!"

He was resolute. "It is too much. James and Tall Mary are very involved with themselves. It is becoming too much for just Petrol and me. It's very difficult."

Even Quincy recognized that both Grace and Petrol came to the Life Boat as residents, needing assistance themselves. She knew they weren't giving up. But Quincy wanted nothing more than to leave them all. Quincy turned and left the room, and when exiting the sacristy, she again felt the coolness of the place. She sat in the middle pew. The silence calmed her. Quincy ignored Grace and Petrol walking down the side aisle, past her.

Before they left, she commanded, "Tell Salvus I want to see him."

She pointed to the pew behind her, "Right here."

Chapter 24

Waiting for Salvus, Quincy had fifteen more minutes than she expected. She was rehearsing what she was going to say to him up until the moment he opened the chapel door. Quincy remained looking forward, at the stained glass image of Christ dying on the cross, centered high above and behind the altar, not really knowing why she was staring, or the meaning of what she was staring at, only to not look back and see Salvus.

He slid into the pew behind Quincy. The chapel remained cool and silent.

"Feeling better?" said Quincy.

Salvus sat back in the pew, draping his arms across the top.

"Yes. Thank you," he said.

"You're not dying then?"

"Not at the moment, no," he said.

"Well, you damn near killed our only priest and I cannot have that," she said.

"It's true then, Father Ford was hearing your confession?"

"I revealed more than I intended," said Salvus, placing his arms across his lap.

"And he believed you, did he?" asked Quincy.

"He didn't say anything. He collapsed to the floor. I called emergency services. And I prayed."

"Why did you say anything to him?" said Quincy. Salvus knelt. His nearness made her tremble. Quincy heard his labored breathing.

"I am sorry," he said.

"Why did you say anything? Wasn't I enough?" she said.

"I believed I was dying soon."

"You don't believe me. I told Father Ford you don't believe me," said Salvus.

"Why are you here?" said Quincy. She felt the coolness was gone.

"Victor send you? Certainly not Stephen."

"Your husband is dead, and yet you speak of him as your Ex," said Salvus.

He continued, "You were never divorced or separated, yet you call him your Ex."

"I ask you the same question Quincy, why are you here? This is the last place anyone would ever believe you would be, anyone in the world. Here at the Life Boat, no one is anyone, not anyone like you. The world knows who you are. Who you are is what so many want. But the world is forgetting you and looking for another, just like you."

Silence resumed for a time. Salvus slid off the kneeler and sat back in the pew.

"Because Stephen is dead, you don't believe anything--because Stephen was all that you believed in," he said.

"Very powerful, your unbelief."

"You believed you were dying, that too was very powerful, unless you are deceiving us," Quincy said.

"No, I am not deceiving you," said Salvus.

"I want the wedding to take place next week and you will finish this construction project," said Quincy.

"Where do I stay?" asked Salvus. Quincy stood up, leaning forward against the next pew and away from Salvus, struggling to remain standing.

"That garden office of yours. I leave that up to you."

"I'll move out today."

"No. Get the construction project finished. If Father Ford returns, you will move to the far end of the new addition," said Quincy.

"I have a wedding to organize in one week. The construction project you initiated has stopped. Too many toilets or some such thing. Elacha is too old and now has to care for her brother."

"I now have to tend to too many toilets," he said.

"Beats too few," said Quincy.

"I want to be here alone, now," she said.

When the door shut closed, as she vomited, Quincy's tears mixed in.

She looked at her pool of vomit and made a commitment to lose weight.

Chapter 25

Tall Mary had never attended a wedding, but James had attended many, none of which were religious. His recollections were hazy, but all were raucous affairs with loud bands and plenty of food, alcohol and drugs, lots of drugs. He couldn't remember any actual exchanging of vows.

Mary kept a wedding picture of her parents. Conrad suggested the wedding dress was to be the same as her mother's. He was surprised his daughter agreed. However, James claimed he loved the dress, and told Mary. Paying for the entire affair was her father's other contribution. The wedding photo and Mary's 3D body scan were all that were required to reproduce the gown, to be delivered on Friday. The difficulty was scanning every woman resident at the Life Boat. All of them were going to be bridesmaids. And all of the men were to be groomsmen. It was, "an everyone or no one kind of wedding," said James, with Mary in agreement. Whether or not that included Salvus remained unknown. Quincy had no intention of being a bridesmaid, much less wearing anything dark navy blue. She still had three and a half pounds left to lose.

"I like black," answered Mary.

"Mary, black is not a wedding color," said Quincy. Both sat behind Quincy's monitor on her desk, looking at pictures of other people's weddings.

"I know that," said Mary.

"The men are all wearing black," said Quincy.

"The bridesmaids are all wearing dark navy blue dresses. Dark, almost black."

"I know that," said Mary.

"That's a lot of black," said Quincy.

"What other color, besides black, do you like?"

Mary pointed at the monitor.

"Those are Cala Lilies," said Quincy, "And yes, you can get them in dark purple, pretty damn close to black."

Along with the deep purple, Quincy ordered plenty of ivory cream Cala Lilies.

Mary then got up. She lifted up her chair and returned it to the small break room adjoining the office.

"Goodbye," said Quincy.

"Bye bye," said Mary, and she left the office.

For the first time since he was hospitalized, Quincy phoned Father Ford.

"You accepting visitors?" asked Quincy. "Your sister tells me you're doing very well."

"You're leaving the hospital on Thursday? That's fine, but Thursday's too late. I'll be there in an hour, along with Elacha and Thoman."

"Yes, we are going to talk about the wedding," said Quincy.

"We'll talk about that, too."

"Yes, and that too. See you soon," said Quincy.

Quincy was on a roll. After stopping by Salvus's room to tell him to move out by Wednesday, Quincy met Elacha and Thoman at the van. Quincy elected to drive. Enroute she thought less about what she'd say to Father Ford than how she was going to behave in the presence of Marjorie Bentham, who Quincy imagined was sure to be by Lonan Ford's bedside, attached like a doting wife.

As she drove to the hospital, Quincy had no reason to view or think about any of the passing surroundings. It was empty between the Life Boat and the miles to where the nearest communities still remained. The building rubble left from demolition had yet to be cleared. Most had left the area. No investors were interested in doing anything with this flat, hot stretch of land. The government leveled all the buildings, shut off water, electricity, sewage— everything but the street lights; they were solar powered. The main six-lane road was recently built, brand new by the region's standards, but since it was rarely traveled anymore, it remained in good condition until the last earthquake.

The Life Boat was a self-operating outpost in a former wide agricultural and suburban spread. There were no more farms, no more businesses. The West Coasters did not need this area for anything. All moved to areas with much better prospects.

What was not leaving Quincy's mind at the moment was how the maintenance upkeep of the Life Boat was to be done. Complete foreign thinking for Quincy. Who maintains the plumbing, electricity, and water?

She'd ask Grace when she got back.

Father Ford's hospital was the closest functioning facility to the Life Boat. West of the hospital, for a five mile stretch, the outcasts spent their lives.

For years there was spasmodic political discourse about building a north to south, three hundred mile wall to separate the coastal region from the rest. But the supposed need never matched the actual threat to those who lived on the coast. Everyone that could, left. Once past the last street of homeless, the good life buzzed, and the look and feel of prosperity rose in propinquity to the Pacific Ocean. From Quincy's residence, a strong cast could reach the ocean during high tide.

The hospital waiting room was sterile white, and quiet. This was the second floor, where admitted patients stayed. Down on the first floor Rule Number

One was strictly enforced. If you wanted to receive medical attention, would-be patients stripped, were chemically washed and deloused, all body hair removed, old clothes destroyed and new brown synthetic clothes put on. They were injected with a formula that guaranteed severe nausea and vomiting if any patient consumed alcohol or certain drugs. (For those that did not stop drug use, dealers enticed them with work around synthetic drugs, specifically designed to avoid the severe nauseous payback.) As a result, most days on the first floor were serene. Only those beat up, gunshot or stabbed—and of those, only the ones that could make it in on their own accord submitted to Rule Number One. The rest stayed on the street. The hospital could at least say they gave Rule Number One patients a chance to make a better choice. Tracking recidivism rates was not necessary. It did not matter.

This zone was used by government and the prosperous West Coasters to demonstrate benevolence both claimed to bestow--with the government taking credit during the periods of attempted property and living tax increases. But when the West Coasters galvanized against these cyclic attempts to further increase the already onerous tax burden, they struck back by cutting government positions—accusing them of being unnecessary—robots could do their jobs. You have to be a double-digit millionaire or better to be a Westie, and if government overreached, the price was very unpleasant. Westies tolerated only so much government, preferring to control the region through health care endowments and philanthropic drug dispersion. Drug them; yet see to their everyday needs. Westies didn't mind the outcasts. In all realms, government still could not compete.

So, the career government types waited for the Big One. The earthquake of earthquakes. An ocean rise that would drown the entire West Coast. Guaranteed government would return in full in the aftermath.

Robots. The government was attempting to populate certain hospitals with medical robots. Under highly experienced supervision, medbots performed very effectively. But the Westies protested medbots from being in *their* hospitals. The compromise was medbots operating only on the first floor of the hospital.

For an hour Quincy waited while Elacha and Thoman visited Lonan Ford. Quincy never was one to constantly reference her PED. Distraction was never a dependency. She had others to perform PED-referencing while she dealt with the business of ensuring total image domination of herself, an

161

extraordinarily competitive endeavor. Before the Life Boat, that was what Quincy did--not much earnings in the first year--but afterwards Quincy's wealth put her in very exclusive company. She had gone global in a flash and was able to remain in demand. They worshipped the transparency of the life and image of Quincy.

Soon she was determining her quest by defining it, in order to make sense of it, searching to find any fulfillment in it, pursuing all opportunities to birth an ultimate sentimental touchstone--herself--for everyone to lay their virtual hands on, invulnerable to the profiteers of scandal, and in so doing, she would become timeless. Quincy could then proclaim she was never forgotten.

Someone once told Quincy that what she really did was leap from soap bubble to soap bubble. They were so perfect in shape, beautiful in their golden luminescence, yet with only seconds of life until they vanished. Right before they popped, Quincy mined the gold and leaped.

But she was unable to leap beyond her husband's death.

Elacha and Thoman exited Lonan's room. Elacha nodded to Quincy to enter. Quincy loathed hospitals. Pale, thinner than Quincy recalled, Lonan Ford was dressed and standing, leaning on the end of his bed.

No Marjorie Bentham by his side.

Lonan Ford said, "Yesterday, I looked out the window and saw an upside down bird on a wire. One foot was mangled, unusable. The other foot grasped the wire and it hung there, upside down. That is what that bird has to do. The bird let go, dropped a few feet but flapping it wings, reorienting head up to fly away."

"This means you will talk to me then, but only in parables?" Quincy noticed his small suitcase on the bed.

"Not a parable, but a witness to a story."

"I love stories. They are the bricks of the house of life."

"You promise to tell me your story--because I cannot make sense of what little I know...and I promise to marry James and Mary, and learn to deal with the presence of Salvus, which defies any sense I thought I possessed."

"To assimilate, you mean," said Quincy.

"Agreed," she said.

Quincy hid her relief. Whether she'd tell him her story--she was undecided. She slid his suitcase off the bed and offered her arm.

"So, he told you didn't he. And you believed him? That's what happened?"

Lonan Ford refused her assistance with a smile.

"Do you understand what his story means?" said

Ford.

"That he is who he says he is? No I'm afraid, I don't feel or understand the magnitude of his admission," said Quincy.

"Put the suitcase down," he said, and he sat down on the bed. She sat next to him.

"It is not the story of who he says he is--and I believe Salvus. His story by itself is a story for the ages. But I collapsed once the significance hit me. My mind seemed to shut down. I felt my heart stop. I had no ability to draw breath. I had no time to think I was dying, right at that moment."

Quincy listened in stillness.

"I dreamed," said Ford. "And when I awoke, the first thing I asked for is my PED. I dictated everything I could remember. But I'm not ready to listen what I said."

"Do you know the significance?" asked Ford, holding Quincy's hand.

Ford's eyes teared.

"It's the closest to understanding His mercy I've ever known. It is still hurting my capacity to understand. A deep physical pain I tell you."

"Infinite mercy. Infinite," he whispered.

In silence, they sat together for some time as Father Lonan Ford wept. Outside his room, an auto-chair was waiting for him. Sitting in the chair, Lonan said aloud, "Forward." The chair rolled to the elevator, with Elacha and Thoman as escorts, and Quincy a few steps behind.

In the elevator Father Ford said to Quincy, "Also, promise you will invite Marjorie Bentham to the wedding. As my guest. She is a very competent medical person. You need her."

Chapter 26

Nearing midnight, in a worn white t-shirt and canvas shorts, his new sneakers set aside; Cart practiced wedding music barefoot on the organ as workers transformed the chapel into a blinding floral whiteness. At the entrance, a ten foot archway of white roses. Hanging on the ends of the pews were oversized bouquets of gardenias with maroon Cala Lilies in the center. Fifty thick, tall white candles were interspersed amongst the multitude of lengthy white slender pedestals of white tulips that crowded both sides of the altar. The air conditioner was set to sixty degrees. Sitting and listening to Cart, Grace thought they looked like a gathering of giant albino asparagus. But Grace was impressed with the pews, the benches now covered with white velvet seat cushions. Petrol was busy assisting the decorators. He loved walking back and forth through the archway, overcome by the fragrance of the roses. When Quincy entered the chapel, Cart segued into a fast boogie-woogie. She had no intention of having anything other than a blinding white chapel for Tall Mary's wedding. And with high satisfaction, Quincy lost the remaining three and a half pounds. Under the white rose archway, with Cart looking up from the organ, Quincy grabbed a wide-eyed Petrol and moved her hips back and forth twice to Cart's groove. Quincy gave the chapel a thorough inspection, and though pleased, was ready for tomorrow to be over today. She figured she couldn't hate this wedding any more than she hated hers. Hated her wedding, loved Stephen.

"I'm going to bed," she told the chapel. With Cart still playing, no one heard her.

Lying down, Quincy soon fell asleep. She dreamt of Stephen. That big galoot of a man, never bothering to have replaced his hair gone long ago, a man who accepted a large waistline as it must be. A man whose inner life he cared for with high regard and cared little who knew. Until he met Quincy, a woman who seemed not to give a damn, other than to dominate the competition. It was a gift for Quincy to discover he was not her competition. She was the only one Stephen wanted to know about his inner life, how his thoughts would range across a polymath's matrix of interests. That's how he knew he loved her. In her dream, Stephen, wearing a luxurious tuxedo she had picked out for him, talked on and on about something he was very excited about. But she couldn't understand what he was saying. He was beaming, flapping his arms up and down, looking like a giant penguin. Quincy awoke laughing. She remembered thinking Stephen was a visiting alien from the other end of the Milky Way. She never knew people had the kind of inner life Stephen had, and the passion to construct a galaxy of thoughts. Stephen also fell for her laconic habit of being. When she was in full control of herself, no one could charm better. This made her even more attractive. But immediately after Stephen died, Quincy became aware that many of her famous mysterious utterances now resembled mere rudeness poorly disguised within trivialities. Quincy had no inner life, relying totally on Stephen's. Her smile was gone. Her mind was empty. She wondered if it was too late to construct an inner life. What would bind it together? What meaning was even worth the effort?

At three in the morning Quincy awoke to a faint cry. Cracking open her door, she watched Olivia, holding an infant, leading Father Price to her old room. She entered, and then Father Price left them and went to his room. The beautiful losers return, with a baby. She thought—they're still living their fantasy?

Enough pondering, it's going to be a long day that she'll wish to forget but won't be able to. That much she knew. No matter, the Syrian priest would marry Tall Mary and James. One last thought--how many marriages had Salvus been the destructor?

Quincy didn't fall asleep, her attempts to keep this thought her last failed.

Chapter 27

The Wedding

Quincy had things to do, to deal with, and say, and nothing focused her in the morning than a lengthy cold shower. It was still early and overcast when Quincy walked to the dining area, thinking of Olivia with infant--Father Price in tow. That Melkite better be ready, she thought, knowing she would be fighting off being bad-tempered for the rest of the day. Then there was Marjorie Bentham. And the Cynths, now six of them operational, all to be in full service during the reception. Today, if she had to hit someone, she could at least bash a Cynth.

That the weather was not hot and sunny, Quincy didn't notice because Marjorie Bentham was already in the dining area, flitting about. Not really flitting, thought Quincy, big women don't flit, but watching Marjorie Bentham she couldn't think of the right description, only serving to swell her ire.

Bentham had been in conversation with Cart, who appeared from the kitchen clutching a hot cup of coffee--unshaven and wearing last night's clothes. Bentham rushed Quincy.

"Are you to tell me that with these women here, with demanding daily needs to be met, you have a resident, Mary, who herself has needs, as the only one to assist them. All of them?" Bentham was out of breath.

"Cart claims you and Mary are a team, and together you take care of them," said Bentham, convinced Cart was lying.

Quincy hadn't thought of her mother in decades. Only Quincy's mother dared to speak to her in this way, and Quincy's memory of her hand stinging after slapping her mother's face remained as sharp as the sting. Behind Bentham sat Cart with his coffee, looking at Quincy through side eyes, shaking his head.

Quincy walked past Bentham to the kitchen to get a cup of coffee. Bentham turned in silence to watch. Next to the coffee maker stood Salvus, adding milk to his.

"When do the caterers arrive?" she asked, waiting until he stepped away from the coffee maker so she could prepare her cup. Salvus never was in the kitchen this early.

"They are on their way," said Salvus, holding up his PED, showing a pulsing blue dot on a map move slowly on the main road to the Life Boat. His body felt as if with flu, and his head ached. He wanted to lie down and rest. But Salvus had slept all night. He knew because of his epic dream.

Tall Mary arrived, on time as always, dressed in

black skinny jeans and black t-shirt. She appeared as though today was any other day, loading the rolling cart with medicines that required refrigeration, and checking the cabinet underneath the cart to make sure all the supplies were there.

"Good morning," Quincy said.

"Good morning," replied Mary. "Time to go."

Together Mary and Quincy left the kitchen, with Mary pushing the cart, passing Cart sipping his coffee, and past Bentham, still standing in the same spot when Quincy walked away. Moments after the two women left the dining area Cart got up and walked past Bentham, saying nothing.

Father Ford and his sister Elacha walked side by side towards the dining area. Ford appeared as strong as Quincy remembered seeing him. Elacha held his arm.

"Salvus is in the kitchen," Quincy said.

"I've told Elacha about Salvus."

"And?"

"She's not sure what to believe."

"What do you think?" asked Elacha.

"When I don't think about Salvus, I'm grateful," said Quincy.

"Father Price and Olivia returned last night. You are still performing the wedding."

Surprised, Father Ford and Elacha turned to watch

Mary and Quincy wait for the elevator.

Going up, Quincy said, "You knew about Father Price and Olivia returning?"

"I kept a secret," said Mary, smiling. "My baby will be as beautiful as Olivia's."

This morning, the women residents were in good spirits and easy to give attention and care. The dresses they were to wear were all hanging on the outside of their closets for them to see; pressed, very pretty, as if showing off, and impatient for the special occasion.

It was this morning when Quincy finally acknowledged to herself the impact of working with Tall Mary. Quincy's acknowledgment came when she realized she was imitating Mary. She spent the past months memorizing how Mary handled each woman in accordance to what she believed they needed that day, the very few words Mary said to them, her tone. And most striking to Quincy was Mary's expression and demeanor, never impatient, never harsh, even during the most trying of circumstance--when the women were exhausted from a night with no sleep, or during times when they cried and screamed in anger, unable to perform a simple function. Quincy never put herself in any position to be exposed to anybody else's suffering. She walked away, out of time and place in order to not be a participant. It was a normal thing to do. That's what everyone does.

But when she decided to marry Stephen there was to be no walking away. The vow was the vow. And she did not walk away from Stephen. At first, she thought he let her off the hook. A fatal heart attack while away on business. Died in his hotel suite, re-reading 'The Last Gentleman", a novel by Walker Percy. But after his burial, after all of Stephen's multitudes of well-wishers faded away, Quincy knew Stephen didn't let her off the hook at all.

Quincy caught up with Mary as she was finishing caring for Catherine. Quincy believed that it was only a simple thought that Catherine wanted to marry Cart. He looked after her during most of the day. Their wedding would not come to be.

"How is James doing this morning?" asked Quincy.

"He's going to talk with the priest."

"Oh?"

"He needs to tell him something," said Mary, letting go of Catherine's hand and saying to her, "Cart is busy practicing music, he'll see you later." Mary wheeled the cart past Quincy and left Catherine's room.

Quincy followed. "You know what he wants to say to Father Ford?"

"James is sad today. It's the same sadness he gets

sometimes."

"Are you sad today, Mary?"

At the elevator, looking up at the floor number 'two' light up, Mary replied, "No."

In the elevator Quincy said, "Do you miss playing in your band? I was going to buy a guitar and get lessons from James."

"No."

Mary looked as focused as Quincy remembered her when Mary was leading her band.

"I'm getting married. I'm going to have a beautiful baby."

She certainly wasn't showing, thought Quincy.

Back in the dining area, Quincy and Mary found an excited Grace and Petrol, talking with Father Price, Olivia, and infant, along with Elacha, Thoman, and the Syrian women residents, very impatient for breakfast. After Mary dropped off the cart in the kitchen, she stopped to view the infant, touching her tiny fingers, the infant clutching Mary's forefinger tight in heightened eagerness. Then Cart joined her to bring the rest of the residents down to breakfast.

"Did we wake you last night?" asked Father Price. "We did get your message."

Quincy said, "What's the baby's name?"

Now Tall Mary's father, Conrad Osborne, walked in, already dressed for the noon wedding.

"Susanna," said Olivia. Olivia looked fabulous thought Quincy, thinking Susanna looked like all infants at that age; bundled in a blanket, all cheeks, no hair, and eyes struggling to blink—not quite ready to take in the world. That will change fast, Quincy thought.

Father Price looked as if he never left. Only once did Quincy's eyes meet his on this morning and he gave a familiar smile, a convincing smile. Whatever inclination Quincy had as to why they left without warning, she no longer cared. She knew they weren't staying. Ash Price was a book Quincy couldn't open, but never attempted to read with any seriousness. If she asked Olivia, Quincy was sure she'd tell her who Ash was and what he was all about. What interested Quincy more was Olivia, and why in this world would she fall in love with a priest, and then have a baby. Former priest she concluded, because they both took the trouble to wear wedding bands. Quincy twirled her own around her finger.

Father Price approached Quincy. Tall Mary and Cart entered the dining area with the rest of the women residents, getting them in place for prayers and breakfast. Grace stood up and delivered a prayer of thanks, for the food, the return of Father Price and Olivia, and to Tall Mary and James.

Quincy and Father Price stood together, to the side.

The Cynths began to serve breakfast.

Quincy said, "You knew I could handle the Life Boat and you knew I would stay, didn't you?"

"What surprised me was that you convinced Olivia not to say anything to me about your leaving."

Price said, "Yes, we knew you could handle the Life Boat, but it was Olivia who convinced me not to say anything. I wanted to tell you everything." They watched everyone eat. Quincy was famished, but those last three and half pounds were not coming back on.

Price continued, "Why do you think Olivia did that? I never asked her why--because there are times I've found not to ask, but I was hoping she'd tell me."

"I am sorry for not telling you beforehand," said Father Price.

"Let me introduce you to someone," said Quincy. He followed her to the kitchen.

Quincy forgot Marjorie Bentham was here. She was talking to Salvus. The Cynths maneuvered around the two, still serving breakfast.

"Salvus, meet Father Ash Price, former director of the Life Boat. Thought you two might get acquainted." As Quincy departed the kitchen, not bothering to look back, she added, "And you know Marjorie Bentham."

Quincy knew better than not to eat. It was going to be a long day. She sat down next to Olivia, who was feeding Susanna. The Cynths were unaccustomed to serving Quincy because she refused to let them.

"Breakfast please, a full plate," announced Quincy to all the Cynths. Moments later she was served a plate full of scrambled egg whites, bacon, potatoes, along with black coffee.

"Do you miss it here?" asked Quincy, while eating. Olivia smiled and nodded.

"I should have had children years ago—three or four," Olivia admitted.

"You never did?" asked Olivia. Quincy continued eating, shaking her head.

"I prevented that option early on," said Quincy, washing down her potatoes with coffee.
Thinking about Salvus, Quincy thought it a better idea to have Olivia meet him--she wanted to know what Olivia thought of Salvus--more so than Father Price.

"Ash is still a priest, and we are married," said Olivia, finishing up feeding Susanna. Tall Mary had been waiting impatiently to hold the infant. Knowing this, Olivia placed Susanna in Mary's arms, giving her simple instructions. Giddy, Mary walked away, whispering to the infant.

"Cake and eat it too?" Quincy finished breakfast as if in a race.

"Yes."

"Congratulations." She turned and watched Mary

walking in slow circles with Susanna.

"You're Catholic now?"

"Oh no," said Olivia.

"Ash couldn't change your mind?"

Olivia smiled, shaking her head.

"I know someone who might," said Quincy, getting up from the table, looking towards the kitchen. The caterers arrived. Quincy joined Conrad Osborne, who was relieved when Quincy stepped in and gave them instructions. The marriage company services included food, beverages, decorations, and a sound system for toasts, announcements, and music entertainment. Grace was serving as emcee and DJ.

Quincy then made her way to the chapel. The sky remained cloud filled. The air--pleasant.

The chapel was refrigerated. All the flowers were vibrant and alert. Quincy was pleased. In the front right pew sitting close together, were Father Ford and James. They were late noticing Quincy walking down the aisle.

Sitting in the pew behind them, she said, "James, you're ready, yes?"

James did not wear worry well.

"We are in confession," said Father Lonan Ford. Quincy stopped just short of rolling her eyes.

"James...your worries are, what?" Quincy, inched forward on the pew, leaning close to him.

179

Not hesitating to share his train of thought with Quincy, James said, "I'm more rather than less a wreck of my own making who was lucky not to go to salvage. I'm a fool. I was foolish."

"But I'm good with all that," he said, "And Mary doesn't know enough to care, and I believe she wouldn't care if she knew. I believe that."

"She's pregnant," said Quincy. Breathing deep, James bent his head down very slow. Quincy rested her chin on top of the pew back. She waited, as did Father Ford, now no longer presiding over confession.

"No," said James, head still low, "No."

"First, we have not done it."

"Second, I know what they do to a woman like her, and so, she can't have a baby."

Quincy's head popped up.

"Let's go James," she commanded.

"I'm not going to see her now!"

"No, you're going to talk to her father. You need to hear from him what he has to say about that," she said, grabbing James's shirt sleeve.

"I'm not going to talk to him, neither!"

Quincy announced, "So, is *now* the right time to call you a lame dick?"

James did not lift his head.

"Father Ford, go and get Conrad. He's the big man

180

in a tuxedo fretting back and forth in the dining area. I'm staying to hear the rest of James's confession." Father Ford asked for forgiveness for wanting to slap Quincy. He got up and left the chapel. As the door shut he stopped to spit on the ground. But he resisted and went to find Tall Mary's father.

"She's not a good bass player," said James.

"Her timing, she has almost none. I can't teach her timing. I tried."

"Don't you need a good drummer for that?" said Quincy.

"She won't play to a metronome. She won't even play to me tapping my foot to a beat."

"Does she really like to play bass?"

"She might just like the sound, or the feel of the bass when she plays the strings. That deep boom, it spreads everywhere, and she's in the middle of it, you feel it deep in your chest. At least I do when I listened to Mary. She didn't look to me to give a damn about playing with anyone. She was playing for herself, to herself."

"Now you're going to be Mary's deep boom," added Quincy.

"She just thinks about the baby," said James, standing up watching Conrad enter the chapel with Father Ford.

"Met him once. Never talked to him."

Quincy and Conrad passed each other in silence.

Leaving Father Ford, she said, "If I ever confess, you'll be the one."

Quincy walked alone from the chapel to the dining area, under graying skies. She swore she smelled humidity in the air.

Entering, Marjorie Bentham ambushed Quincy. "Tell me you are not going to get these women dolled up for this."

"It's an important day today. We're all going to look smashing," said Quincy, watching the caterers setting up and decorating. Bentham stepped in front of Quincy.

"This is not your dollhouse, and these women are not your playthings."

"You're wearing a nice dress for the wedding too, yes?" asked Quincy.

"I don't have time to wear dresses," said Bentham.

"But you're making time today, yes? Otherwise, why are you here?"

"Father Ford pleaded that I come."

"Women wear dresses to weddings," said Quincy, seeing Tall Mary and Olivia still sitting together, both attending to Olivia's baby.

For the first time, Quincy noticed Bentham's plain gold wedding band. So slim, over a thick finger.

"You wore a dress when you were married?" With difficulty, Bentham shoved her left hand in her tight jean pocket.

"I usually help Tall Mary care for the women, but today, you'll help me instead," said Quincy, staring at Bentham. Bentham stepped aside.

Quincy peeked into the kitchen. Father Price was still listening to Salvus. She asked Grace and Petrol to begin taking the women residents back to their rooms. Following them, Quincy looked at Bentham, unwilling but accustomed to being alone, standing near the dining area door. Quincy motioned to Bentham to follow them, not waiting to see if she consented.

Bentham watched Quincy, who said little to the women as she tended to them, only smiling and thanking them for helping her help them. Quincy combed their hair as Tall Mary insisted they liked their hair to be combed. Each woman had a preferred perfume. Quincy had no idea where the perfume came from. She dabbed behind their ears, and on both sides of their necks. Clear lip-gloss was Quincy's only makeup contribution.

Short Mary talked to Quincy, asking where Tall Mary was, and could they have a party too. Short Mary, Louisa, and Anne were ambulatory, but walked with difficulty. Catherine, Anne and Rachel walked with such difficulty they needed wheelchairs. Of them all, Catherine talked the least, but seemed to comprehend the most. Anne and Rachel only spoke in one or two word phrases. Eye contact was crucial in communicating with all the women.

While getting the women ready, Quincy and Bentham said nothing to each other. When they finished Quincy said, "My turn. The wedding starts in two hours. Plenty of time."

She left Bentham at the elevator and went to her room. On her desk, in a bucket of ice, a bottle of champagne chilled. The note was from Grace. It read, 'See you at the wedding!' For the reception, Quincy ordered ten cases of Stephen's favorite, and because of him, Quincy's too. She grabbed the bottle and walked quickly to the elevator, but Bentham was not there. Quincy raced down the stairs to the parking lot.

"Take this. Drive safe," she said, placing the champagne in Bentham's hands.

The silence between them was very uncomfortable for Marjorie Bentham. Not for Quincy. She fetched another bottle of champagne from the kitchen and returned to her room. As she left the empty dining area, she noted the decorative transformation--any decoration was an improvement. The place still looked like a neglected school of the old days.

Chapter 28

It was noon. Ready were Mary and James, the priests (Father Price joined Father Ford, evidently a 'priest' thing, Quincy was told), and a tuxedoed and shaven Cart bent over the organ. Quincy swore at some time, he may have been handsome. Plus, everyone else, and everyone looked spectacular, thought Quincy. She only had three glasses of champagne. Steady rain had been falling since the end of breakfast. Fifty flickering tall candles substituted for the day-in, day-out sunshine normally beaming through the stained glass windows. Amongst the tall tulips, Salvus observed the solemnity created by the candlelight. He thought the sunlight's radiance yielded giddy optimism, mostly unwarranted. Either way didn't matter to him. He was distracted by the weight of an aching weakness. Sitting alone in the back of the chapel, Salvus looked shades worse than Mary's father. Salvus was a sallow stick figure swallowed in a black suit.

Susanna napped in Olivia's arms. The women residents had yet to begin their fidgetiness. To the left of the arch of fabulous flowers, stood Conrad Osborne, sweating—next to him, Mary. He should have had at least two glasses of something, thought

Quincy, standing to their far left, noting the only person missing was Marjorie Bentham.

Then, in the second row, Catherine collapsed. Her head was cushioned by Louisa's lap. Cart's attention diverted to Catherine. As he watched Louisa's eyes widen, her reddening face contorted in panic as she slid away from Catherine, her limp head resting on the new velvet cushion atop the pew. Like everyone else, the other women residents in the same pew were unaware. Quincy could not get Cart's attention to start the procession music. She marched down the left aisle to the front, waving at him. Then Marjorie Bentham entered the chapel. Cart looked up, noticing her dress and matching hat made Bentham look like a wide hipped dandelion, framed under the arch of white roses. Just before Louisa cried out, Cart began to play. On cue, Father Ford, Father Price, and James exited the vestibule and stood in front of the altar. Everyone who could rose from the pews. Across the chapel, Quincy saw Catherine lying on the pew, with Louisa crying. She marched to the back of the chapel, not quite believing what Marjorie Bentham was wearing, and pushed Bentham down the right aisle. Cart flubbed a note. Conrad was whisking his daughter down the center aisle. Quincy noticed and stopped, catching his attention with a look of menace. She moved her hands to slow down. Conrad obeyed.

As Conrad and Mary stopped in front of James and the priests, Bentham easily scooped up Catherine, and in maneuvering past Quincy, pressed her hard against a Station of the Cross figure set hanging on the wall. Bentham hustled up the aisle and left the chapel. Those who watched Bentham carrying Catherine as she clomped up the side aisle were unsure what they were seeing. Then they all stared at Quincy. Quincy gave Cart the same look of menace she gave Conrad. Cart continued to play without any further mistakes. No need to give the look to Father Ford--he saw Quincy look at Cart. Father Price smiled. Conrad presented Mary Osborne, both unaware Catherine collapsed, into the arms of James. As beautiful as she could be, Mary was. Grace moved to slide into the pew next to Louisa. She calmed in his comfort.

Salvus wanted to follow Bentham and Catherine out, but he remained standing, holding the top of the pew to steady him. Shivering, he thought he might have a dangerous fever.

Father Ford began. Quincy returned to the back of the chapel. Seeing Salvus, she decided in a flash of a moment to sit next to him. Whether wanting to not think about Salvus, or to continue grieving for Stephen, her own wedding appeared in her mind's eye. It was on a Greek island, she couldn't recall which, Patmos maybe, and the ceremony took place in a very small, whitewashed chapel. Stephen had it all arranged.

Quincy was no longer in the Life Boat chapel, now remembering the shimmering sunlight blinding against the whitewash walls and blazing through the stained glass windows. The loud blue roofs, hot and dry—every single day. Then an arranged demonstration of how the Greeks burned clamshells to produce lime paste and mixed in sand to form the white wash to cover the thick, cooling volcanic stone used to build their homes, and everything else.

Inside the Greek chapel it was a contemplative coolness, just like the Life Boat chapel, Quincy admitted. Her fitted wedding dress was royalty cream, short, sleeveless—with intricate gossamer lace overlay. Their fat priest wore a long beard. The only persons present were Theo and Elissa, Stephen's frail parents, and Victor. Stephen and Victor went back to their early youth. Quincy didn't know if Victor was married. They were all practicing Greek Orthodox. Only by the requirements of the Orthodox to verify Quincy's baptism did Quincy discover she was baptized Catholic. Her parents never went to church, never talked about anything religious, never hinted at belief in God. Quincy always seemed to know they were never a family, merely a man and woman living together in near perfect marital dysfunction, with a girl also living with them. This arrangement set in volcanic stone Quincy's attitudes towards marriage and children. (Quincy never said she was from a family, only that she was from an arrangement.)

Stephen changed her mind towards marriage because thinking of him in part caused her to cease thinking about her mother. Rather than dismiss with pungent sanctimony the concept of marriage, Quincy believed the only way to know anything about marriage was to marry. And at age fifty Quincy married Stephen, ten years older, and up to then a bachelor, more by unconscious detachment than rakish determination. He was taller than the five foot ten Quincy, but not by much, obliquely handsome with no distracting features, what remaining hair was more salt than pepper, unconcerned with his physique, but adamant about his attire. Everything tailored, casual wear was only black slacks and flawless white shirts—finest cottons, or silk, or cotton and silk blends, sometimes rolled up to just below the elbow. His accents were shoes and glasses. Being drawn to experimental fashion, designers fought for Stephen's attention.

Both were so well known their marital union was a global phenomenon for almost two months. Stephen shunned attention to the extreme; Quincy's business relied on the complete opposite.

If Stephen had dominated the media business instead of his business realm, having extraordinary control on the what-how-and-when Celeb content was revealed to the public, he said he would have served Quincy's business endeavors like a gun barrel to a bullet. Stephen wanted no part of Quincy's business because, as he told her, her business was to penetrate the willing with herself. And she was recognized for how extraordinarily well she accomplished that on her own.

Yet, without hesitation and overwhelming surprise to herself, she agreed to marry Stephen. Her self-surprise seemed to serve as the final say on her decision. Shortly afterwards she was further surprised how quickly she lost interest in her business. Quincy then discovered she loved the extraction game more than the attention game. And with supreme calculation, she extracted herself from attention seeking, stealthily, precisely on her schedule of amusement. Stephen only observed. He knew it was her gift to him. Instead of finding a successor, Quincy slipped out of the game of Celeb cultivation, and her competitors are fighting for her flag, continuing to fight amongst themselves for domination, so far, none succeeding like Quincy. It was her gamble, and until Stephen died, she was the winner.

While not away on business, Stephen attended Mass at the Life Boat. During that time Quincy practiced staying thin, and yoga. Though she thought he never intended for her to reside at the Life Boat, Stephen requested she visit if he died, perhaps for a few days, and of course she would have never thought of not consenting, more because of her unwavering belief in the high improbability of his death than her love for him. Love had little to do with her consent she thought at the time. She discovered afterwards the depth of her delusion.

But now, after almost two years of marriage, and his death seven months ago, Quincy knew the truth mattered little because at the Life Boat no one knew how brief their marriage was and how recent Stephen died, except Olivia and Father Price. And of course, Salvus.

Father Ford pronounced James and Mary man and wife, and after their nervous kiss, more a quick series of pecks, Petrol led the applause, and everyone joined in. Mary and James looked as if they would need an escort out of the chapel. Petrol bounced from the pew and hugged them together. Only then did Mary smile and James's stiffness slacken. Everyone cheered. The women residents were unsure what to do, and those that were able clapped and yelled. But they all were excited to toss up silver and gold confetti and watch it float about, and after the serene descent, squeal in laughter as it settled on them and everyone else. Mary insisted. The glitter reminded James of naughty past times.

When Mary and James were half way down the aisle Quincy said to Salvus, "I'm here because I kept my promise to Stephen. Your question is answered-- and if you're as sick as you look, Bentham can prescribe you something I'm sure."

Cart began to play some fast boogie woogie. Grace was in charge of photography. He realized in an instant he was not going to get all the proper photographs of the bride and groom under the floral arch, and also amidst the tall candles and tulips around the altar. Seeing Grace panic, Quincy stepped into the aisle, motioned Grace to come to the back of the chapel, circled behind Mary and James, firmly guiding them to turn around under the floral archway, and whispering in James's ear. Quincy motioned Grace to come forward. Quincy stood aside and Grace let the camera do the work, taking rapid, multiple pictures.

"Smile!" commanded Quincy.

With hands to their backs, Quincy pushed the couple back down the aisle and placed them at the altar. Cart shifted into a sublime rendition of "When a

Man Loves a Woman." Only some of the very old knew that song, but James and Cart knew it well. James had insisted. Grace aimed and took picture bursts as Elacha helped Quincy get the women residents up to the altar and gathered about Mary and James--and the fifty flaming candles amongst the tall tulips. Olivia handed Susanna over to Ash and joined in helping Quincy and Elacha. Quincy shoved a bewildered Conrad next to his daughter Mary, commanding him that he too, smile.

Petrol kept stepping in front of the wedding party. He couldn't wait to give James his present.

"Open it, open it!" yelled Petrol, pressing the small white, gold ribbon adorned box in James's hands.

"Just push the top of the box down, push the top down!" said Petrol. The women residents had become irritated. The confusion of the photo shoot overwhelmed them.

"Push the top down, push the top down!" cried Petrol. James gave in and pushed.

"WARNING! WARNING! TAKE PRECAUTION! BULLSHIT DETECTED!"
Petrol fell on the ground in hysterics. Cart stepped over him, rushing out of the chapel. His new dress shoes still under the organ. Catherine wouldn't notice.

Chapter 29

"I'm not sure what happened in the chapel, but Catherine seems much better," said Marjorie Bentham. Cart's presence was the reason for Catherine's smile. He arched his neck as far as he could manage, nodding to Marjorie Bentham.

"You're welcome Cart," she said.

"A much better place for you here, obviously," she said, looking around the dining area, the catering staff milling about, now observing the Cynths, all awaiting the wedding party.

"For a lotta people," said Cart.

"I didn't know you were a musician," she said. Cart held Catherine's hand.

Marjorie Bentham left to assist the other women residents getting to the wedding reception. Walking to the chapel, a flash of memory of her own wedding came upon her. While her memories of the ceremony and reception were not worth remembering, marrying her husband was the most important event of her life, and she refused to say to anyone otherwise, no matter the perceived sacrilege of that fact.

Arm in arm, Mary and James strolled passed Marjorie Bentham--Mary in a hurry, James slowing her pace.

"Congratulations," Marjorie said to them, conjuring up a smile. She meant it. She wished them every bit of satisfaction they could ever hope to attain. But smiling was just something Marjorie never had call to do anymore, and she was ashamed the habit had become permanent.

James gave a nervous smile.

Twenty minutes later, everyone was settled in, the women residents sitting where they always sat. While everyone came in and sat down the caterers finished transferring all the tall candles and tulips from the chapel into the reception area, surrounding the section reserved for dancing. Petrol helped re-light the candles. Grace dimmed the room lights to where the room turned into a stage where the wonderful dreams are portrayed.

Grace the DJ played a luscious organ recording of "Arrival of the Queen of Sheba," by G. F. Handel. Then in strolled Mary and James, both smiling, Mary because of what was to happen next, and James, enjoying Handel that he requested, knowing he was the only one familiar with the piece. Perhaps Salvus also, James thought, and maybe Conrad. Mary then watched silver and gold glitter float down from the ceiling. Small sparks erupted as they touched candlelight.

Olivia led the clapping, and then everyone joined

in. Looking up, the women screamed with delight trying to catch the glitter. Petrol appeared at the door. Above his head, he waved Cart's new shoes. Petrol ran and dropped them in front of Cart. Soon Grace began Mozart's Symphony No. 40 in G minor K. 550, very popular with all the women residents.

Conrad beat everyone to the champagne. Marjorie could not recall when she was with other women, all in dresses, in sparkle, or glitter. Before she began her work in the district--before she began her search on the streets.

The caterers served everyone champagne. Conrad gave a toast to the couple, followed by Olivia, and finally James to Mary. Everyone cheered. Now that the glitter had settled, the Cynths, their round chrome tops dusted in silver and gold flecks, reflecting every candle, began serving the courses. Elacha and her Syrian women, along with Thoman, sat at a separate table. Father Lonan chatted with Father Ash, each trying to wipe the glitter from their suits.

Conrad sat on the opposite side of the large round table from Salvus. Marjorie didn't know where to place herself, finally choosing to sit next to Conrad. Feigned smiles were exchanged, although Conrad's champagne brain was starting to lighten up a bit. Color returned to his face.

After confirming the caterers had control of the

reception, Quincy looked out from the kitchen door, sipping champagne. To sit as far from Marjorie Bentham as possible, but at the same table, Quincy had to sit next to Salvus, whose skin now was such that she thought she might see the ice water he sipped spill through his mouth, down his neck, and into his gut.

No one noticed Quincy as she made her way to the table. She sat down. Surprised, Salvus choked on an ice cube.

"No champagne?" asked Quincy, to Salvus.

"I'm unsure that's wise," he said.

"You feel ill, again?" she said.

"I don't feel well at all," he said.

"Look, first have a glass of champagne. It is the best, I tell you," she said, adding, "Then some prime rib, two thick slices, and some potatoes with butter. To look at you, I don't think you need any albino asparagus, although they are fantastic."

Barely audible was Coltrane's "A Love Supreme." Quincy recognized the record. One of Stephen's favorites. She looked over to James, much more relaxed, smiling, his head nodding to Elvin Jones's genius rhythm. He was looking at Mary, again holding Olivia's baby.

"Congratulations Conrad," said Quincy, her glass held high towards him. She pointed to a wandering glittered caterer and motioned to serve champagne to her table companions.

Coltrane's frenzied saxophone solo now sounded as if he was in urgent, inaudible conversation. Grace faded out the record like a pro. He had been practicing. On to Bill Evans, live at the Village Vanguard, 1961.

James was directing the musical selections with timed glances to Grace.

With his glass now filled, Conrad returned Quincy's gesture. Marjorie Bentham pushed back from the table, big legs crossed, arms folded in her lap.

Salvus stared at his full champagne glass. Quincy reached over, grabbed his glass, and raised it towards him. His eyes followed the glass, up from the table over to inches in front of him. His eyes traced the length of Quincy's arm and then looked at Quincy. She was not as surprised as she feared. His eyes were as she expected them to be. Salvus accepted the glass.

"Mrs. Bentham, join us," said Quincy turning away from Salvus--a moment's eye to him was long enough.

"My name's Conrad," extending his hand to Marjorie Bentham. After hesitating, she uncrossed her legs, and picked up her glass.

"A toast to James and Mary," said Conrad. He finished his glass.

"To James and Mary," repeated Quincy. The

yellow dress and hat Bentham wore, she might be staring now, Quincy thought, but that color yellow, with some kind of green neck trim, it made her look like—Quincy buried the image. Marjorie Bentham and Salvus lifted their glasses as if conjoined, saying nothing, then sipped.

Quincy swore Cart looked less bent as he wobbled to their table, his head up and cheeks flushed, taking a seat next to Marjorie Bentham. Accompanying him was a full glass of champagne. Quincy couldn't remember if he was an alcoholic. One drink does not fall a man, thought Quincy. She swore she just experienced a sense of worry. That thought too was buried. Marjorie Bentham smiled. Her teeth were flash white, much to Quincy's relief, for worry they may have matched her dress.

Salvus finished his champagne. He cut into a thick portion of prime rib. Quincy swore his color was changing. She motioned a gold flecked caterer to refill his glass.

Across the table, Cart engaged with Marjorie Bentham. Her laugh, thought Quincy.

Conrad wore the smile of a relieved drunk.

To the left of Grace stood Ash and Lonan in deep conversation--Lonan forced to look up at an almost extreme angle at the much taller American priest. Quincy didn't care what they were talking about.

Turning to Salvus, Quincy asked, "And?"

"A welcome recommendation," he said, now extra buttering his potatoes.

Pellets pinging—the sound from above--rain was arriving in torrents.

Cynths were motoring about picking up plates, knives, forks, and spoons.

Cart was entertaining the Giant Dandelion.

Quincy was forgetting to eat.

James motioned to Grace the DJ. Time to dance.

Mary and James danced by themselves to a lovely melody that no one recognized. Mary had never before heard any of the music played, and while being led by James in their wedding dance, she gave him a goofy thumbs up, accompanied with an approving smile. James kissed her cheek.

Quincy watched them intently, as did Marjorie Bentham--Cart having left her to rejoin with Catherine.

Salvus smelled the rain. Careful not to admit, he smiled to himself, very cautious to acknowledge he was feeling better--lest he be deceived.

Conrad danced with his daughter. Awkward. Quincy wanted to know what they were saying to one another.

Next came the Korean pop songs. Bouncy and saturated in thin synths, strangely accurate English pronunciations, immersed in a deep beat. With experience, Grace and Petrol corralled all the women residents to the dance floor, along with Mary and James. A new dance was created.

Offset by themselves twirled bent Cart and Catherine in swivel chairs. After minutes, Cart spun Catherine back to their table for a rest. She sipped from his champagne glass that he held for her. Cart made his second move.

Surprising Quincy, he rolled up to her with an empty swivel chair.

Without hesitation Quincy sat in the chair and rolled with Cart to the dance floor. The music changed to the Temptations. Quincy was enjoying being silly in their chair dance swirl.

As the tune began to fade, Cart swung close and said, "Marjorie Bentham has spent ten years looking for her husband on the streets. That is why she's been out there. No other reason. Now you give her some respect."

"Her husband's gone...we knew him, but not as her husband. He walked away from their home-- schizophrenic as the damned days are long. We couldn't do much. She never knew why. She never found him."

Cart forced his neck up as far as the sharp pain allowed, staring at Quincy. "Consider commiserating, with less of a bitch face." He then spun away, back to Catherine.

During Quincy's chair dance Salvus had talked with James, afterwards approached Grace. Grace received an affirmative nod from James and a few moments later changed the music to Shostakovich's Waltz No. 2.

Quincy was where Cart left her, alone on the edge of the dance floor, in a swivel chair, dazed--between tall candles shrinking, losing their wax down the sides.

Salvus approached Quincy, extending his hand.

"A dance?"

"With..?" said Quincy.

"Not necessary," said Salvus, cutting her off.

"You can lead," said Salvus, his color now closer to the middle of prime rib.

"That's a man's duty," she said.

"Duty?" he asked.

"Yes."

She then asked, "Well?"

"I will lead," he said. Quincy accepted his warm hand. She was never aware of his deep calluses. From the moment she lifted herself from the chair, Salvus led. His command of dance was absent any unnecessary movement, with full cognizance of rhythm and flow, each move seamless with the previous and the next. She was now alert, but unsure her shivering would cease.

"I see that Stephen accomplished what I believed I was supposed to," said Salvus. He was no longer stiff-necked and appeared to enjoy dancing.

"I'm supposed to know what that means," she said, noticing everyone approach the dance floor. Everyone, but Grace and Petrol. They stood together behind the DJ console, deciding what to play next. Petrol had no clue, but no one knew, his look that serious.

"Does that mean you failed?" asked Quincy. Salvus's arms were thin, yet sinewy. His command of the waltz was flawless. With little pressure, her hand could feel the back of his ribcage.

"I learned something here, at the Life Boat. I'm not the one to answer that," he said.
Conrad and Marjorie Bentham glided by. No longer awkward, Conrad missed dancing. In Conrad's arms Quincy did not see a Giant Dandelion.

"I don't really have to say anything to you, do I?" said Quincy, avoiding eye contact, missing
 Salvus's slow rise smile.

"Infinite mercy--that's why Father Ford told me he collapsed. That mean something to you?"
Salvus was continuing to smile as he twirled Quincy about.

Finally, he said, "Oh yes."

"You don't have anything else to say to me, do you?" said Quincy.

"I would like to have met Stephen," he said. That Salvus never did, relieved Quincy.

Next passing by came Mary and James. Late at night in his room, under earphones, James had taught Mary to waltz, or at least not to prevent him from leading. Although Quincy was no longer aware, she continued to shiver.

"Yes, well--I would have liked to dance with him today," said Quincy.

The arrival of the towered wedding cake announced the end of the waltz.

"You are an excellent dancer Salvus," said Quincy, releasing herself from him.

Salvus gave a short quick bow.

James led Mary to their cake and together they sliced their piece. The caterers soon had a piece of wedding cake in front of everyone. Olivia led the cheers.

Quincy sat down with the women residents, who by now were all exhausted. Short Mary and Louisa were asleep. Catherine remained awake only because Cart remained close, talking to her. Anne and Rachel were quiet but crying. Quincy stood and pulled her chair over to sit between them. She alternated smiling at Anne and Rachel, offering each a bite of cake from their plates. Neither was interested. Quincy took a bite from Rachel's portion. Enough sugar to cause immediate onset of diabetes, thought Quincy, as her shivering ceased. She remained with the women until Mary and James finished their cake and posing for pictures by Grace.

Leaving their cake untouched, Elacha, Father Lonan, and Thoman left to settle the Syrian women to their rooms.

Mary then noticed the miserable Anne and Rachel. Handing James her plate, her cake uneaten, she went over to them. Now Olivia joined her, and together they delivered Anne and Rachel to their rooms. Quincy remained sitting, watching.

Next Cart assisted Catherine to her room.

"She'll need you to get her ready for bed," said Cart to Quincy.

Quincy followed behind Cart wheeling Catherine out of the reception. Later, Mary and Olivia brought Short Mary and Louisa to their rooms.

For hours, thunder followed the lightening, brighter than anyone could remember. Again and again the rain came heavy.

Each of the fifty tall candles offered nimble auras throughout the evening and into the early morning, as if protecting Quincy, who, after a while, returned to sit alone.

Chapter 30

Today was shaping up to be the same as the Wedding Day, almost a year ago. Since that day rain had become more frequent. La Nina, El Nino, bastard son of weird weather, unwanted daughter of temperamental sunshine, Quincy couldn't guess, or care, because she never was a fair weather fisherman. Quincy fished to catch fish, and on most days, eat them. She was out dark early this morning, with twelve rod and reels, one by one testing them for worthiness.

While leaning each fishing pole against the pier railing, using her headlamp for light, Quincy began to speak: "I know who won't be there this Sunday. Mary and James's honeymoon started off the day after the wedding sitting in premier seats on the maiden ride of the VacTrain, courtesy of me of course, and Mary's second most important dream fulfilled. I remember that morning was a mad scramble to get them out of the Life Boat. They packed in less than fifteen minutes, I'm sure forgetting most things they wished they hadn't."

"Do you like the blown up and framed electronic postcard I showed you from them? You know, the two of them, with two goofy smiles with the Golden Gate

Bridge in the backdrop--on a blustery day? Mary's hair was whipped up and about, certified out of control. She needs a gargantuan hair clip for that mane of hers. The postcard said they arrived in San Francisco an hour and a half after departing from Los Angeles, just as they claimed it would."

"Of course, Father Price, Olivia, and baby Susanna are gone—no, not in Thailand anymore. You know Stephen, it's funny--Ash is the one to keep in touch. A small area of China, Catholics thrive for some strange reason. That's where they are, in a province I can't pronounce, much less recognize in writing, only that it starts with "Q", and Ash thought that was hilarious...I showed you the latest pictures they sent, didn't I?" How many times Quincy talked of these stories, she would never admit.

All the reels operated as they were supposed to. Quincy rigged each for pier fishing, using live bait. She returned each rod and reel into a handled carrying contraption, six per contraption, alternating the reel end fore and aft for a balanced load. She could have accomplished this at home on the back lawn, in daylight. But Quincy wanted them all tested on the pier; with the ocean water anointing each one. A sunrise baptism, she thought, must have some significance.

She returned to her van, walking passed the predawn regulars in silence, recognizing everyone by their general height, shape, the hat they wore, and their rigs, but knowing no one.

"Home please, Stephen," she said, once inside and ready to go. The van started, the headlights switched on, the inside light dimmed slowly, and the transmission settled into reverse. Moments later the van pulled out onto the main road, and as the orange streaked dawn arose, Quincy drifted asleep.

She awoke once inside the garage. She was too comfortable to move just yet. In the kitchen the coffee was just about ready, and while imagining its aroma, Quincy became aware her shower was turning on, the water temperature would be perfect.

In slow motion, she opened the passenger van door, and hopped down. Entering the kitchen, the lights rose at a leisurely rate. She took off her backpack and placed it on the countertop next to her coffee cup.

"Good morning, Miss Fisher Lady," said the voice of Stephen. His hologram appeared next to the refrigerator. Dressed in pressed black slacks and a crisp white shirt, sleeves rolled up once. Quincy preferred him barefoot.

"Good morning, Stephen. No fish today, just checking out some new rigs," she said.

"Not even a bite?" said Stephen. The likeness was

uncanny.

"Not this morning," she said, pouring her coffee. While sipping, she pried off her left boot by toeing the heel, removing the right boot with her hand. She continued to undress in the kitchen. In her undergarments, Quincy sipped her coffee walking to the bedroom.

"I'm going to shower," she said.

"May I join you?" said Stephen.

"Love to have you but that's not the best idea," she said. As she entered the bedroom, Stephen's hologram appeared.

"You sure?" he asked.

"Not the best idea, Stephen, I'm telling you...but love the thought," she said, leaving her coffee cup next to the sink and entering the shower.

"Beautiful!" said Stephen as Quincy exited the bathroom.

"Thank you, Stephen."

She put on makeup and dressed.

"I should join you," said Stephen, appearing in the kitchen.

"I know. See you in a while," she said.

"I love you!" said Stephen. Quincy entered the garage.

In the van, she said, "To Mass please."

It was soon after Quincy programmed her van to

accept commands upon saying Stephen's name that she got the idea—just after leaving the Life Boat, while beginning her travels. She mentioned it to Victor once, merely as a--what if? He accompanied her on the overseas ventures, Cuba, Iceland, Patmos, and Patagonia. Merely a traveling companion. Victor arranged everything.

In Cuba, she recalled saying to Victor, "What if I had a hologram of Stephen? The quality is amazing." She'd swear she was just musing aloud, forgotten soon after mentioning.

But Victor did not forget.

The first day with Stephen's image and voice was as if experiencing a toxic shock dream. This was to be expected, according to the Hologram Company. The first night she couldn't sleep, for fear of hearing his voice, or worse, wanting to. The next days were all queasy--putting effort into normalizing an unreality, assimilating Stephen's image and voice back into her life. To commit to a delusion--and all the effort the delusion demands to make it soundproof against any screaming doubt. But after a month Stephen's hologram only had the effect of leeching her deep love for him. She couldn't imagine any other effect it could have; no matter how popular they were with the Westies. But she couldn't let it go. What a failure. Stephen would have been appalled. That Quincy had started talking to him aloud--if he knew. Stephen would have begun to share her extraordinary state of sadness. What a dismal failure.

****

To Quincy, everything looked the same driving east. The same streets--where those that would not or could not leave survived--and the same sprawling emptiness. Only until reaching the Life Boat, the changes now left the place unrecognizable. The parking lot was expanded and secure with high walls, cameras, and a solid gate, with a facial scanner for authorized entry. Guests had to call in advance, including the few parents and relatives who still attended Mass on Sunday.

Quincy arrived early. She had been attending Mass after quitting her travels. Unloading the fishing poles, she carried them to the storage room behind the dining area, unlocking the door with her fingerprint and voice. She placed them next to the other poles she had donated, now twenty-four in all. A wall rack had been installed for the poles, just like in Quincy's garage.

In the chapel, she sat in the same pew where she sat for the wedding—next to Salvus, who left the day after Quincy, so far not returning, although Quincy gave explicit orders to leave his room untouched. She sat in silence. Praying remained an unnatural effort. Quincy knew the prayers, knew how to pray the rosary, she could not see the point in all that repetition. She did keep to her one short prayer--said every morning and evening, and lately given to repeating it over and over, unconscious of her actions.

Father Lonan Ford led her through all the requirements to become a Catholic. But first she demanded to know what else Salvus told him that led to Father Ford's collapse.

"He did not talk about you," he said.

"But what can you tell me?"

"I can tell you to read the Gospels. Read what Jesus says. Think about what Jesus says. And pray for understanding about God's mercy--the gift of gifts."

Quincy was a terrible Catechumen. Whether out of spite for Father Ford not revealing the conversation with Salvus or not compelled in any way to try.

"I have told you that Salvus came to the Life Boat because of me," she said.

"A number of times now," said Ford.

"I only vomited twice. But you were hospitalized," she said.

"Maybe, maybe he came here because of you," said Quincy. Father Ford had thought of that many times. But for Quincy to say that, well, that was something else to contemplate.

She still smiled when recalling her first Confession. None could confess like Salvus, Father Ford did tell her, but she ranked second, even though gratefully he emphasized, a chasm of distance second. Four hours she spent with Father Lonan Ford, face to face, telling her life story through the sins she committed. Father Ford earned a pounding headache listening for any hint of contrition. Afterwards, he admitted he was deceiving himself when he detected remorse. What Lonan Ford remembered from the experience was not that in confessing she couldn't be as fully contrite as she was expected to, because she made it clear she dealt with some terrible people throughout her life. What he remembered was Quincy felt bad she slapped her mother so hard--but Quincy was convinced her guilt, if that is what it *must* be called, was only due to her mother being dead.

****

Now Father Ford appeared from the vestibule. He returned Quincy's greeting as he made his way around the altar--a last minute inspection. Over the next few minutes, Elacha and Thoman brought the Syrian women residents in, along with the other

Syrians who were part of their original group when they immigrated. They decided they were better off with Lonan and Elacha. In total, they filled half the chapel.

Grace and Petrol looked the same; maybe more gray hair. After helping Anne, Rachel, and Catherine in their pews (Monique, Veronica and Rachel's parents, Anne's mother, and Catherine's much older brother still attended), Grace and Petrol stopped by and each gave a peck on Quincy's cheeks. Short Mary died soon after the wedding. Other than the Syrians, no new residents had arrived since Quincy left. There weren't that many left in the region, maybe none at all. No one knew with any certainty. Their complete absence was part of the culture now.

The Life Boat was what Stephen asked Quincy to consider, and only because of him did she come. Was it not the mission, the place in and of itself? Was it a place strange enough to somehow warrant an attempt to pause her life, and maybe her grief would transform into a scarring acceptance? If so, futile. Why?

She missed Grace and Petrol, Mary and James.

One of the new Syrian women played organ, as Cart had become very frail. He entered in his wheelchair, pushed by Marjorie Bentham. The only time Marjorie wore a dress was to Sunday Mass.

Running the Life Boat was really a blue jeans and t-shirt operation, maybe a flannel shirt in December and January.

It was Cart who persuaded Marjorie to select certain ones from the street to be a new resident. But so far, each newcomer came with relationships developed on the streets, and those relationships were contagious, and destructive. They clung to what they had, regardless of the outcome. None of them lasted a week. It did not matter if they had their own room, shower, clean clothes, meals, and some labor required of them setting up and tearing down the Life Boat stands at the fresh markets, selling vegetables and herbs the successful garden produced. Cart was dejected, but Marjorie would have none of it. She made him come with her back to the streets. They were going to find someone who was a good fit, but there was no certainty in any selection criteria. They spent enough time on the streets to know better. The few they remembered being likely candidates were gone. To search--it was an ingrained habit of sorrow Marjorie felt she must bear. To do otherwise she feared, might lead to despair.

And there was Catherine. After Mary and James left, her enthusiasm for Cart left too.

Cart was relieved.

Quincy stayed afterwards only long enough to

have a cup of coffee in the dining area, deliver harsh glares to the two Cynths White and Gray, and listen to Grace and Petrol tell their stories of the week. She told them she put twelve new rod and reels in the storage, and they agreed to plan a fishing trip soon. Quincy and Marjorie Bentham managed to say, "Good Morning", and nothing more. Father Lonan said little, and when asked, Elacha would talk with enthusiasm about the success of the Life Boat's new venture, selling their produce at local markets.

Back at home; Quincy was greeted by the image of Stephen.

"Back so soon?" he said.

"I did stay for a cup of coffee."

"How was the homily?" he said.

"You would have enjoyed it I think."

"I'm going to change and sit outside, get some sun."

"Good idea Quincy, it's a beautiful day today," said Stephen.

The sun never quite overcame the low clouds. Outside, Quincy shivered in damp grayness. Every minute of waiting felt like an hour. She was also starving but couldn't go back inside. It would soon be over, it would soon be over, she kept repeating.

Waiting. Shivering.

Then the doorbell. She avoided going back in the

house and instead ran around to the side gate, slowing to an urgent walk to the front door. Her shivering only increased.

Today was the day.

It had to be done. Stephen would offer her his profound thanks.

In the driveway there was an additional van. One was from the Hologram Company, and the technicians were still inside the van.

Quincy heard the doorbell ring. It was Mary, with James waiting dutifully by her side.

Trembling, Quincy shouted their names.

The Hologram Company technicians looked up and got out of their van.

James turned around. When Mary turned, Quincy saw something cradled in her right arm.

"Aunt Quincy! I want to show you my beautiful baby!"